"REFLECTIONS"

By Lori L. Howell

ISBN: 978-1-61750-755-7

DEDICATION

To Michele DeArruda and Laura Bottini, my daughters, my grandchildren, and Barbara Lundquist, my mother, family and friends-for their love and support through this spellbinding journey; and always to God for my blessings!

Chapter One

At St. Teresa's Hospital in Atlanta, Georgia, a child is brought into the emergency room. She is doubled over in pain and emotionless. Fluid is dripping down her legs and there's a puddle on the floor. What she doesn't know is that her water has broken, and, in any moment, she would become a mother.

Alayna Dupree is fourteen years old, a child having a child. She gave birth to an eight-pound-nine-ounce baby boy. He is a beautiful child with smooth, peachy skin, dark brown silky hair, and the features of a baby angel. He enters his new life with a soft whimper, his dark gray eyes barely peeking through their tiny slits. It is amazing that Alayna, weighing 100 pounds when wet, could give birth to a child of his size.

Ella Jackson, the pediatric nurse, is a large hardy black woman. Her smile and voice displays her sincere love and compassion. Her fashion style isn't the typical nurses uniform decorated with an apron and a surgical cap worn as a bandana. One would think she is Aunt Jemima from the Old South. There is something extraordinary about Ella. She has the most loving and compassionate heart with a patient and gentle soul.

Ella is an adopted child. Her mother was young and was forced to place her in adoption. This explains her compassion in trying to reach young mothers. She hopes that after the mother saw her beautiful baby, with the feel of its flesh and the smell of her own scent as she snuggled her nose into its cheek, she will then decide to keep her child.

Ella instantly becomes fond of Alayna and her new baby boy. There is something about this teenage mother that will leave a lifelong emotional hold on Ella, *a disturbing haunt.*

She leans towards Alayna to put the baby on her breast for nursing, love, and comfort. Alayna shakes her head from side to side, with stone-cold dark blue eyes giving a loud message; no. The nurse felt chills up her spine, deep and frightening. She now is experiencing the cliché. They say that the eyes are the path to one's soul, a mirror reflection of their inner self.

"Child, this is your son, a beautiful boy," exclaims Nurse Ella. "Don't you want to hold him before you give him away?" she asks.

Ella is persistent. She knows that Alayna has signed papers giving the hospital permission to give her son up for adoption. But she is in hopes that Alayna will, at least, feel some emotional connection with her baby boy. Ella wonders what this baby felt during the nine months growing in his mother's womb, nestled next to her heart.

Was it the warmth of love or a dark empty coldness?

There is no response from Alayna. She turns away and closes her eyes. Ella kisses the baby's forehead as she puts him back in the bassinette. She looks at him with such heartfelt pity and sorrow. She reads his foot tag: "Baby Boy Doe."

"Well, my little man, this just will not do," declares Ella.

Ella picks up a blank foot tag and a bright red marker, writes "Abraham Lincoln," and replaces the foot tag "Baby Boy Doe."

"He freed the blacks from slavery. And there are all types of slavery. I name you Abraham Lincoln (Abe) in hopes to free you from a horrible start in life, free of evil. I saw the evil in your mama's eyes!"

"Abe may you have the freedom to live a loving life," expresses Ella.

Ella pushes the bassinette holding Baby Abe into the nursery and caresses his tiny hands and feet. As she walks away, she prays that God will bring some loving and wonderful parents to adopt Abe and hopes that Baby Abe will never be in a foster care program.

The next day, Alayna gets dressed and packs her life's belongings in a backpack. She walks a few blocks out of sight of the hospital. She then hitched a ride to the bus terminal and buys a ticket to Mississippi, not her preference. This is all she can afford and she still has to leave her a little money for some food. She isn't too concerned about where she will live. The streets are her family; she spent many years living from rat hole to rat hole, a safe haven. To Alayna, this is more of a loving place than at home with her stepfather and stepbrother.

"Ella, I wanted to give you some blessed news. I know you have been extremely concerned about Baby Boy Doe," says Head Nurse Sandy Boston. Sandy Boston is Ella's supervisor. There are three nurses in pediatrics, and, with the nursing staff being short handed, Ella eagerly works as much overtime as possible. This has become Ella's home away from home since the death of her husband.

"Please call him Abe," Ella insists.

"Ella, listen, there is a couple coming in this afternoon to sign the adoption papers. They were waiting to adopt another baby earlier this morning, but the baby was delivered stillborn. God works in such mysterious ways. They are wonderful people. They want Baby Abe," says Nurse Sandy.

"I think the name you gave him turned his fate. You're a blessing to have at St. Teresa's," Nurse Sandy excitedly says.

"Oh! I must tell his mama," exclaims Ella.

"I don't think she cares," replies Nurse Sandy.

Ella walks into Alayna's room. She calls Alayna; no answer. She checks the bathroom; the room is empty. There is no sign of Alayna or her belongings. Ella's heart sinks with despair.

"Sweet Jesus, help this child," Ella prays.

Chapter Two

The Children's Protective Services arrives as Ella is leaving Alayna's room. Ella knows this is routine because Alayna Dupree is a minor. They must investigate the possibility that she has been abused and protect her rights as a child. It is their job to determine where she is from, her family background, schools, and how she wound up pregnant, staggering into St. Teresa's Hospital.

"Hello Ella, I am Melanie Carson, the social worker handling Alayna's case. Can you tell me anything about her that might help me understand this young girl?"

"There really isn't much to say. Alayna came to the hospital two days ago, gave birth, signed the adoption papers for her son, and, before being released, she left on her own," Ella remarks in a disappointed tone.

"She never said a word the whole time she was here. Alayna is so young to have such a cold, broken spirit. And she is stunning with her big dark blue eyes, creamy white skin, and long blond curls," describes Ella.

"And, Ms. Melanie, there was an unnerving sense of evil in her eyes."

"Thank you, Ms. Ella. I will contact you when we have anything on Alayna," Melanie responds as she walks towards the exit door of the hospital.

"Please do, I am holding you to your word." Ella's voice is quivering; masking her tears.

Chapter Three

Seven years later…

Ella is visiting her ailing mother in Nashville, Tennessee. She switches channels on the remote control, and, while flipping through the various stations, a news flash comes across on KSBW Channel 49 from Nashville, Tennessee.

"There has been a sad, but a long awaited end to the capture of a serial killer. This serial killer has been at large for seven years. The first murder was in Georgia, four in Mississippi, and the last three in Tennessee. This case was solved with the brilliant help of Dr. Bailey Fairchild, a forensic pathologist. Dr. Fairchild was called on the case and has done an outstanding job using her forensic expertise," narrates reporter Lauren LaMont.

Ms. LaMont starts an interview with Dr. Fairchild.

"Dr. Fairchild, I know you have put a large amount of your time and heart into this case. I was hoping you would elaborate on a statement you made. You said it was the overdose of evil that was fed throughout Alayna Dupree's life. It was the overdose of evil by men that drove her to become a serial killer and then to be murdered," Ms. LaMont quotes.

"I will start with the facts of who she was and her life of hell."

"Her name is Alayna Dupree. Her mother died when she was eight years old. She was left to her stepfather to be raised. She was molested over and over again by her stepfather and stepbrother. At fourteen, she gave birth to her son. The DNA analysis proves that the stepfather is the father," explains Dr. Fairchild.

"How can you be so sure that it was her stepfather?" Ms. LaMont asks.

"Through the Atlanta, Georgia Police Department sources, they were able to get Alayna's home address. And, because she was a minor, the police department was granted a warrant to search her home. During this search, the crime team collected various samples that proved the stepfather's DNA analysis was a perfect match to her son. Both the stepfather and stepbrother have disappeared, leaving no trace of their existence," elaborates Dr. Fairchild.

"Alayna made her life on the streets, prostituting from the time she was fourteen until her capture. The men whom Alayna encountered were very abusive to her. She snapped, and, in pure defense for her safety, she killed them," says Dr. Fairchild.

"When the detective tried to persuade Alayna into surrendering, she attacked another officer and was shot," explains Dr. Fairchild.

"Every human being has the characteristics, emotions, and motives of being transformed into something beyond their own imagination," declares Dr. Fairchild.

"Are you justifying her being a serial killer?" Ms. LaMont asks.

"No, it's so important to have a consciousness—awareness toward each other's feelings and state of mind. We are humans and we all have a breaking point," says Dr. Fairchild.

"Alayna endured years of physical pain and emotional torture. Love was never in the equation," explains Dr. Fairchild.

"Dr. Fairchild, thank you for this interview and congratulations in closing this case. Will you be working on any other case?" Ms. LaMont asks.

"I think I will be taking some time off. This has been a long and emotional case," Dr. Fairchild exclaims.

"Dr. Fairchild, I am curious, do you know what happened to her son?" Ms. LaMont asks.

"He was adopted by a very loving and respectable family. I understand he is doing quite well," Dr. Fairchild says.

Chapter Four

Dr. Fairchild straddles her long legs around the sides of a chair in her study, pulls her laptop towards the center of the desk, opens the laptop, and proceeds typing.

The next day, Dr. Fairchild mails her resignation to the Board of the Coroners and Medical Examiners Office, emphasizing "effective immediately."

* * *

Ella screams in disbelief to her mother.

"Oh, my God, that is what happened to Abe's mother."

Chapter Five

The Forensic Pathologist Conference in Toronto reads across the two-day conference agenda. Dr. Fairchild prepares for her lecture to be held in two weeks at the University of Toronto. She is honored that Dr. Charles Ralston will be a guest speaker at the conference.

Dr. Ralston has devoted his life to the study, teaching, and advancement of forensic science. He has worked for decades as a professor at the University of Lyons in France, has participated in numerous forensic investigations, and has been an expert at many criminal trials.

He comes from a very wealthy family. His grandfather was an oil tycoon, and his father inherited the wealth.

When Dr. Ralston confirms that his topic would be on "*An Integrated Perspective on Death Investigation/DNA Identification and Mass Killings,*" she knows that this will be an informative and interesting conference, probably one of her best lectures.

Dr. Fairchild agrees to meet with him after the conference is over, a little curious at first, but decides not to read more into his request.

These two colleagues have much in common, even more than Dr. Fairchild realizes.

Chapter Six

It's three o'clock in the morning. Dr. Charles Ralston is unable to sleep. He jumps abruptly from bed as though a firecracker was suddenly lit in his pajamas. He remembers that tomorrow is the deadline for the Forensics Anthropology Conference at the University of Toronto. Dr. Ralston is more intrigued in meeting the famous Dr. Bailey Fairchild rather than his topic that he is brilliantly known and respected for. Normally, as a forensic pathologist himself, the topics at these conferences will be his first passion. But this conference is very different. What he is about to learn is knowledge that will only impact his life and future, not for anyone else attending.

He shuffles his feet under the bed, trying to slide them into the upside down slippers. After a few seconds of shuffling, his mission is accomplished.

Dr. Ralston shakes the teapot to make sure there is enough water before he turns the stove on. He waffles in his flip-flop slippers to his office that is around the corner from the small but conveniently located kitchen. He pulls back his leather computer chair and sits in front of his large teak wood desk. Even after ten years, the desk still has that deep sweet teak wood aroma. He presses the ON button of his computer and waits patiently for the monitor to open. The teapot whistles for someone's attention. Charles waffles to the stove and pours the very hot water into his forensic mug. It's quite a unique looking mug. It leans to one side and is crooked, with big red letters "ME" printed on the front and back. He also wonders what particular message was being sent by his wife, who gave this to him on his first ME lab job.

He opens his e-mail and scrolls to the registration form that was sent by Dr. Fairchild. The e-mail was sent a month earlier. But he wasn't sure if he was going to attend at that time until he downloaded the hyperlink to the Forensic Pathology Lecture website, and, on one click, a picture of Dr. Bailey Fairchild appeared in the midst of an article where she was discussing briefly what topics will be covered during the two-day conference. Intriguing, to say the least, he decided this would also be a great opportunity for his son, Anthony, to come along.

Dr. Ralston has relatives in Canada who haven't seen Anthony. And now that Anthony will be starting his first year at Harvard, he feels that this will be a perfect time to reunite with his family and take a break from his marriage; something that both he and his son desperately need. Since their only child is leaving for college, his wife is having difficulties with the empty-nest syndrome. Therefore, her mood swings and nasty temper flares more frequently than usual. Dr. Ralston completes the registration form, and, in the body of the e-mail, requests for the opportunity to meet Dr. Fairchild after the conference to discuss the Tennessee serial killer case. He then books their flight and makes hotel reservations.

The next day, he personally receives an e-mail from Dr. Fairchild acknowledging that she would be honored to meet with him after the conference has been concluded.

Chapter Seven

Dr. Fairchild sets up the podium for the lecturers and anticipates her meeting with Dr. Charles Ralston.

"Bailey, I just received a phone call. There is some horrible news. The plane that Dr. Ralston and his son were on crashed while leaving the runway. There were no survivors," Libby reports.

"Do you want me to cancel the conference?"

"No, it would be too complicated. I'll announce the tragedy before we start the conference.

"Libby, Dr. Ralston is from France. Please contact the University of Lyons and find out what we can do for his family. Send a card and flowers. This is a priority," Dr. Fairchild's voice quivers while she tries not to show her grief.

Chapter Eight

In the present…

There is an obnoxious knock on the windowpane adjacent to the door of the forensic anthropologist's office.

"Come in," grumbles Dr. Bailey Fairchild. Dr. Fairchild is a forensic anthropologist in the Laboratoire de Sciences Judiciaries et de Medecine Legale for the province of Quebec. Dr. Fairchild also holds lectures on forensic anthropology at the University of North Carolina at Charlotte and Criminal Justice at Rutgers, The State University of New Jersey in Newark. She also wrote an award-winning thesis on "Skeletal Biology/Hominid Paleontology." Therefore, she has earned the renowned reputation as an expert in this field.

Dr. Fairchild tries to avoid eye contact with Libby, hoping Libby will take the initiative to resolve whatever is causing a distraction from her deadline.

"Dr. Fairchild, you have a call on line one," Libby announces. The irresistible power of Libby's gimlet gray eyes captures and traps you into giving her your undivided attention. It is always impossible to resist Libby. Libby banks on this successful form of manipulation.

Dr. Fairchild looks up at Libby, shrugging her shoulders.

"Who is it?" Dr. Fairchild asks, annoyed. "You know I am on a deadline for the DA's office."

"I know," reassures Libby, "It's Korey Scott. He said it's urgent. It's regarding a body that was found in South Jersey, something about cranberry bogs."

"Thanks, tell him I will be right there," Dr. Fairchild orders.

"Mr. Scott, Dr. Fairchild will be right with you. I would approach her with caution," warns Libby.

Korey puts his feet on the credenza behind his chair, knowing how long a minute can be for Dr. Fairchild, and taps a sharpened pencil over and over again, flipping from eraser to lead tip in a continuous motion on the notebook that contains the gruesome information that he needs to discuss with Dr. Fairchild.

Korey Scott is a colleague that is working on his doctorate in criminology. He works closely with Dr. Fairchild in collecting research data and maintaining criminal analysis reports and is in charge of the preliminary investigations at the crime scenes. He is too attractive to be thought of as a nerd, but his mannerism imply differently.

Korey is six feet three inches tall, with a perfect physique that body builders only dream of. His distinguished looks are accented with jet black wavy hair and sparkling emerald green eyes. Even the heavy, plain black glasses complement Korey's stunning looks. There isn't anything that could make him look less than breathtaking.

"Thanks for holding, this is Dr. Fairchild."

"Why the formalities?" Korey asks.

"I'm sorry, Korey, it's this damned DA. He wants me to give a press release in two days. I am not comfortable with the case. There's a lot of politics, and I believe it is too soon. I don't have all the data back from the ME lab," Dr. Fairchild snaps.

"Is it the same DA whom you had an on again and off again relationship with for how long?" Korey asks.

"You can be such a jerk. You know it was for five years! And, yes, it is Perry Sinclair," Dr. Fairchild replies, annoyed.

"Enough of me."

"What's so urgent that you are calling me from New Jersey on a Friday night?" Dr. Fairchild asks.

"A body was found in the wetlands. It's the swollen red bumps all over the torso that has the medical examiner stumped," says Korey.

"Korey, are these bumps anywhere else on the victim?" Dr. Fairchild asks.

"No, that's the puzzling part. According to the medical examiner, most of the body is decomposed, except the torso, as if it was preserved. There is more. It's decapitated."

"Hmm, interesting." Dr. Fairchild exhales. "Did the medical examiner mention if an autopsy was performed?" Dr. Fairchild asks.

"I didn't ask. She only mentioned the missing parts and the large red bumps all over the torso. According to the medical examiner, the body has been in the wetlands for at least two months."

13

"So, why am I needed for this case? You know I am retired, and I'm focusing more on lectures," says Dr. Fairchild.

"The medical examiner thought of you. She felt this was more your expertise. This is actually her first in-depth case. She graduated from the University in North Carolina in Charlotte three years ago, a professor of anatomy and forensic pathology, and this is her first medical examiner job. You were her professor," Korey explains.

"She remembers the young serial killer in Tennessee and your interview with KSBW Channel 49 seven years ago."

"Who is she?" Dr. Fairchild asks.

"Dr. Katherine Kendall," replies Korey.

"If I remember correctly, she should have no problem drawing the conclusions to this case. Dr. Kendall excelled in forensic science and criminal law, and she challenged my theories throughout her studies. She is an expert in the forensic reconstruction of any crime scene procedures and was one of my most brilliant students. I can't imagine Dr. Kendall having any problems," says Dr. Fairchild.

"Dr. Kendall is getting pressure from the mayor to get this particular case wrapped up, and he doesn't want her to report anything to the press," replies Korey.

"She called me and asked if I could get a message to you, emphasizing the urgency, and how she would appreciate a call within forty-eight hours.

"Bailey, Dr. Kendall didn't sound right. I heard more in her voice than just her lack of experience or confidence in the procedures of this case. She seemed timid, almost scared," Korey expresses.

"All right, I will catch an afternoon flight tomorrow out of Toronto."

"I was banking on that. I already have your flight booked, and I will pick you up at the Atlantic City airport at 11:00 p.m. at the baggage carousel.

"You are on Canadian Air, Flight 1127. I am faxing over the itinerary as we speak. I will see you tomorrow night," says Korey.

"That was extremely presumptuous on your part," declares Dr. Fairchild.

"What if I decided not to go or if I had other appointments that I couldn't reschedule?" Dr. Fairchild asks.

"I took the liberty to have Libby check your business and personal calendar. It was in my favor that you have Libby managing both," says Korey.

Libby calls Perry Sinclair and is able to manipulate him into taking on the press release. He tells Libby that if Dr. Fairchild will send him what she is going to cover, he will handle it.

"You are so obnoxious." Dr. Fairchild chuckles.

"That's why we work so well together." Korey laughs.

"*Well, Bailey, there went any time for your personal life. What life?*" she mutters to herself.

Chapter Nine

Dr. Katherine Kendall is typing a report on the findings from the crime scene. She will be more convinced of the true outcome of this case if she has the assistance of Dr. Fairchild. Dr. Kendall details every aspect of the findings, answering crucial questions that will unveil the murderer, a monster.

She writes her report in detail. She answers many questions that are of valuable assistance to the authorities in finding this monster. The remains are human. Decomposition of the body is approximately two months. The bones and flesh are of one human being. The remains are that of an adult female between twenty and forty years old. Her height is approximately five feet five inches and weighs about one hundred twenty-five pounds.

All details have been recorded and tagged with information from the scene and the processes of the reconstruction at the mortuary and laboratory. The delimitations of the body have been concluded by the results of laboratory testing from the gallstones, fingernails, torso, and bone remains.

A considerable time was spent at the crime scene by the lab technicians and Dr. Kendall, who documented the activity of earthworms that were found a few centimeters around the cranberry bogs and the wetlands. The remains were properly paper bagged, labelled, photographed, and recorded at the crime scene. Dr. Kendall's final step was labeling all evidence "Jane Doe case #0804NJ."

She wonders how one can get used to these grotesque and senseless deaths day after day.

Maybe it's fatigue or the pressure from the mayor that has me in such dismay, Dr. Kendall speculates. *How can a beautiful world be embraced by so much evil?*

Her thoughts are abruptly interrupted by her cell phone ringing.

"Hello, this is Dr. Kendall."

"Dr. Kendall, good afternoon, this is Dr. Bailey Fairchild."

"Oh, Dr. Fairchild. Thanks for calling. I am hoping you will be able to come to New Jersey and help with the final phase of the autopsy of a body that was found in the wetlands."

"Dr. Kendall, do you know who discovered the body?" Dr. Fairchild asks.

"Yes. A horticulturist group discovered the body. They went to the wetlands to study the cranberry bogs. The body was covered with cranberry bogs and was almost overlooked due to the bogs being at full bloom. The body was swimming in a sea of red blossoms," replies Dr. Kendall.

"Were you able to get any physical evidence at the scene?"

"I have gathered and paper bagged over a hundred pieces of evidence, including twenty plastic bags of bogs, water samples, debris, and mud around the perimeters of the wetlands, as well as the embankment," replies Dr. Kendall

"It sounds as if you have covered the preliminary basis. You have performed pretty much of the autopsy, why am I needed?" Dr. Fairchild asks.

"I am puzzled by the preservation of the abdominal area. It just doesn't make any sense what caused the red swollen bumps. The torso is covered with these bumps. I am guessing hives or a rash," says Dr. Kendall in a confused tone.

"And I was able to determine that she had a recent abortion."

"Do you think this was the cause of death?" Dr. Fairchild asks.

"No! It was a clean and very meticulous surgery. I would say performed by an experienced surgeon," Dr. Kendall answers.

"Dr. Kendall, I will be in New Jersey tomorrow evening and will be available the following afternoon. I can meet you in your office around 3:00 p.m. Is that a good time for you?" Dr. Fairchild asks.

"Yes, I will see you then. Do you know where my office is?" Dr. Kendall asks.

"It's 1333 Atlantic Avenue, 6th Floor?" replies Dr. Fairchild.

"That's it. They have moved me to the back due to the renovation. To get to my office, go up the outside stairs off Grand," answers a relieved Dr. Kendall.

Chapter Ten

After they hung up, Dr. Fairchild calls Schwartz Deli. She orders a tourtière and a grande café au lait with extra cream for pickup. As she puts back the receiver, she glances at the silver-plated clock next to the phone, thinking eight o'clock at night is pretty late for a café au lait. After seeing her reflection, she feels sorry for the next person whom she might run into. *Bailey, you are looking tired and unattractive, too tired to care.* But that little bit of vanity always seems to kick in.

Spending too much time on rearranging a barrette from one side to the other, she has given it one last swirl and then clips the dangling auburn curl across the left temple. She gives one last glance at the clock. After examining her reflection, she concludes that she needs to add a melon color lipstick; she begins feeling attractive once again.

She grabs her purse and heads for the elevator down the hall, pushes the "down" arrow button, and waits impatiently for the elevator to rise from floor one to the fifteenth floor, her floor. She paces back and forth in an area no larger than a three-foot radius. Each floor seems to take an eternity. Finally, the elevator doors open. Dr. Fairchild dashes to get in the elevator and pushes "B" for the basement level. The doors open and she walks briskly from the elevator to stall L4. She clicks her key lock; the lights blink three times. She releases the locks and the black Mercedes awaits her entrance. Her body relaxes as she sits and turns into the car. The new smell of the leather interior stimulates the sensual side of her. Dr. Fairchild locks the door and puts on her seat belt.

She fumbles and drops the keys on the floor after trying to insert one into the ignition. Reclining to a sit-up position, she catches a glimpse of a person running in front of the car and then disappearing into the dark parking garage. She starts the engine and the music from the stereo plays Frank Sinatra's top hits. She shifts the car into reverse, then drive, and notices, as she is driving to the exit, that there is a

Lori Howell

shadow of a large man hiding behind the cement columns; she dismisses her sighting. Dr. Fairchild taps on the steering wheel to the beat of the many songs being played continuously as she turns left onto Route 68 towards Schwartz Deli. She was anticipating her dinner from Schwartz Deli and the thought of a very hot bath. Reminiscing about the aroma of the cucumber melon bubbles gives her a second wind for a late evening.

Fortunately, she has been able to park in front of the deli; most times it's an average of a half-mile walk. Tonight was not the time to walk the distance. She was just too tired.

"Hello, Bailey, it's been awhile!" Mr. Paulo Schwartz greets her excitedly.

"Good evening, I know it's been a long time. I have been traveling and solving way too many cases. Whenever I need some home cooking and the feeling of a cozy atmosphere, I always come back here," says Dr. Fairchild.

"Yum, the tourtière smells heavenly and mouthwatering." Dr. Fairchild holds back a drool.

"I thought you were retiring?" Mr. Schwartz asks.

"So did I," Dr. Fairchild replies.

"On your account tonight?" Mr. Schwartz asks.

"Yes, you're a peach." Dr. Fairchild winks with a flirtatious smile.

***

Dr. Fairchild juggles her dinner and grabs her mail from the white antique mailbox while opening the French doors to her French Victorian condo. She stumbles over her gorgeous cat a long-haired Maine coon as she enters the foyer.

"Mousey, tripping me wouldn't be a very good idea," warns Dr. Fairchild.

"I thought I let her out this morning," she murmurs to herself.

"Hello, sweet kitty, I missed you, too."

"Are you hungry, maybe just a little bit?"

Mousey swirls around in and out of Dr. Fairchild's legs, its long gray tail tickling her with every swirl.

"There's crunchies in your bowl," says Dr. Fairchild. Nudging and purring impatiently, wanting to get a taste of that inviting aroma of Dr. Fairchild's dinner, Mousey has no intentions of eating her cat food.

Dr. Fairchild puts her dinner on a Victorian lap table, places her mail next to her dinner, and heads for her bedroom. She fluffs a couple of oversize goose-down pillows and nestles them behind her lower back. She puts the Victorian bed table across her lap, gently lifts the cup to her lips, and licks the hot cream from the top of the café au lait. Savoring every bite of the tourtière, she agrees with Canada's number one food critic, Jean-Pierre Claudel, when he says that Schwartz Deli's meat pie, spiced with cloves and onions, is the best.

Mousey jumps up on the bed and starts licking the cream from the café au lait, while staring at the little piece of the tourtière remaining on the dish. Dr. Fairchild pushes the dish towards Mousey as she gets up to investigate the noise at the back door, a noise as if someone knocked over something on the back porch. Dr. Fairchild's eyes widens with alarm in disbelief that a silhouette of a large man is shadowing through the window shade. She reaches for the lamp on the sofa table and taps the base twice that puts her in darkness. As she feels her way to the kitchen, there's a flash of light and pounding that swarms in her head. Her body drops, and as she lands towards the floor, she looks up and captures the silhouette figure standing at her feet. She tastes something sticky and warm.

Dr. Fairchild's last thoughts before passing out: observe and remember.

Chapter Eleven

Dr. Fairchild feels throbbing pain to her head, and the restraints on her wrists burn each time she moves them behind her back. She is coiled up in a fetal position on the floor, her ankles tied with boat rope. Her heart pounds rapidly from the adrenaline of fear.

She flips from her back to her side, trying to pull her feet through the loop between her wrists. Realizing after many attempts that this isn't going to work, Dr. Fairchild gets to her knees and hops to her feet. She hops to the phone; it's pulled from the wall outlet. She's feeling nauseous and light-headed.

"I have to get help!" Dr. Fairchild cries out.

"Where's my cell phone?" Dr. Fairchild's voice is quivering. She finds her cell phone on the nightstand; she puts a pencil in her mouth and presses number "1" to speed dial Libby.

"Hello, this is Libby!"

"Libby, it's Bailey. Please come to my condo. Don't ask any questions, just get here."

"Do you still have a key to my condo?" Dr. Fairchild asks frantically.

"Yes, I will be there in fifteen minutes," answers Libby.

There's a jiggle at the front door as Libby inserts the key to Dr. Fairchild's condo. Libby opens the French doors to see Dr. Fairchild standing in the foyer with her hands tied behind her back and her ankles tied. Blood has been dripping down the side of her mouth after she bit her lip while falling to the floor.

Libby walks over to Dr. Fairchild and starts untying the rope from her wrists and ankles. Libby motions Dr. Fairchild to the bathroom, grabs a washcloth, and proceeds to gently wash the blood from her face. Dabbing the cut on her lip with a cold compress, Libby sees the fear in Dr. Fairchild's eyes. Dr. Fairchild leans her head into Libby's chest and weeps uncontrollably.

"Bailey, are you okay?" Libby asks compassionately. "My God, what happened?"

Dr. Fairchild goes over the event with Libby, explaining that she has absolutely no idea of why or who.

"Libby, I have to get ready to catch a flight to Atlantic City. I have only three hours to get packed and get to the airport. Will you help me?" Dr. Fairchild asks.

"After all of this? You can't be serious you still want to go!" Libby shouts.

"I feel okay. A slight headache, a puffy lip, and a set of puffy eyes to match," Dr. Fairchild says as she chuckles.

"I guess so, but it's against my better judgment," replies Libby.

"There's one thing. Promise me you won't say a word to Korey," demands Dr. Fairchild.

"Bailey! Is this gruesome case worth all of this?" Libby asks.

"I don't understand the magnetic power forensics have over you."

"I mean it, Libby. Not a word!"

"Sure, whatever." Libby sighs shaking her head in disgust.

"It's a good thing the weather in New Jersey requires long sleeves. I would suggest you wear one of your blouses to cover those marks on your wrists. Or you will have some explaining to do to Korey," states Libby.

"Thanks, Libby, you are the best!" Dr. Fairchild says with a smile.

"Bailey, how did the intruder get in?" Libby asks.

"The back door I am assuming," responds Dr. Fairchild.

"I don't think so," declares Libby. "Look, the back door is locked."

"You know, Libby, he was standing at my feet. That means he came from that direction."

Dr. Fairchild is pointing towards the bedroom, which is adjacent to the laundry room. Libby walks to the laundry room and notices that the window is broken.

"Bailey, you said you heard a noise in the back porch," says Libby.

"That's right," responds Dr. Fairchild. "There's only one explanation. The intruder had an accomplice," says Dr. Fairchild.

"The silhouette was a distraction for me. I noticed that when I came in, Mousey was in the house and I thought I let her out. I wasn't really sure. There has been so much going on. I am in and out of the condo like patients in a doctor's office," responds Dr. Fairchild.

"Bailey, this means he was in the condo when you came home." In a chilling tone, Libby responds, "And, are you sure it was a man?"

"Most definitely. When I was passing out, there was a distinctive odd odor. It's been haunting me. He smelt of a sweet stale cigar. He stood with his arms folded across each other, smirking, watching my body go limp with a look of satisfaction, admiring his deed. What a monster!" Dr. Fairchild explodes.

"Do you know what they were after?" Libby asks.

"I'm not sure. He took my notes regarding this case in New Jersey. And my laptop is gone," says Dr. Fairchild in a disturbing tone.

"Well, I've learned from my last incident. I don't keep anything valuable on the laptop. I type the notes, make a copy to a CD, and leave them at the office."

"What about the notes?" Libby asks.

"There wasn't much. I don't think that's what they were after. I feel it was a warning. I could have been hurt a lot worse.

"Libby, thanks for setting up the press release with Perry Sinclair," says Dr. Fairchild.

"I will call Mr. Sinclair after I take you to the airport to confirm if he wants me to mail the documents or bring them to his office.

"Actually, I would like to restate that I am going to strongly suggest that I should drop off those documents. About now, I need an attractive distraction. He is so good-looking. Those big brown bedroom eyes make my panties wet, and the thought of touching his sexy physique puts goose bumps all over my body," expresses Libby.

"Any other time, I would be a little bit worried about you. And I agree, maybe it's what you need to get past this moment." Dr. Fairchild raises her right eyebrow with a smile.

"Are you planning to stay in New Jersey for an eternity?" Libby asks. "You have packed enough clothes to get you through the winter."

"Funny, a little exaggeration here?" responds Dr. Fairchild. "I am not sure how long this case is going to take. I have a feeling that there will be more to this case than what is being disclosed. It is so gruesome, and yet it is being handled by the mayor with such a rush to close.

"Libby, will you be able to watch Mousey for me? There is enough food to get you through the winter, in case I am gone that long," Dr. Fairchild says with an attitude. "I have written down the emergency numbers and I will leave the pad on the counter. Mousey's vet has my credit card information on file in case of an emergency."

Libby and Dr. Fairchild finish packing the three pieces of luggage. They stack them securely on top of each other, balancing on the luggage rack.

Libby grabs the handle and pulls them through the front door to the trunk of the car.

Dr. Fairchild pets Mousey on the head and scoots her out the French doors. She jiggles the doorknobs to confirm they are locked.

Chapter Twelve

The drive to the airport is unusually quiet and intense. Both Libby and Dr. Fairchild are adrift in their daydreams, avoiding reality, resisting any thoughts that will try to replay Dr. Fairchild's almost deadly encounter in their minds.

To keep her mind occupied, Dr. Fairchild turns on her cell phone to check for any messages; new voice message scrolls across the menu screen. Dr. Fairchild punches in her secret code to play back the message. She presses number "2" to save and turns off the cell phone.

I can't deal with this now, she thinks while glaring at Libby.

Libby's thoughts are on manipulating more time with Perry Sinclair and contemplating if she will seriously act on any further advances that he might have towards her. She knows she wouldn't go there, but she already has. Libby is torn. She has the highest utmost respect towards Dr. Fairchild. Libby feels that even though Dr. Fairchild professes over and over again that she is over Perry, she knows that Dr. Fairchild is still in love with him. The many disappointments and betrayals afflicted by Perry have become a mask for Dr. Fairchild. It is the only way she can deal with the burning pain that is buried so deep within her heart.

Dr. Fairchild places her head against the headrest and shuts her eyes, trying to avoid any thoughts of her almost deadly encounter and the voice message. She focuses on her past relationship with Perry, how he tossed her heart and their relationship out of his life like yesterday's garbage, and the numerous disappointments she allowed the men in her life to deliver. She realizes that this is the result of giving too much in a relationship and not setting boundaries.

Her deepest love is Perry Sinclair. They dated five years off and on. This is the only time Dr. Fairchild allows herself to embrace these feelings, almost in hopes to overcome the fear that the attacker may come back.

Will I ever stop feeling this deep emptiness when I think of Perry? She tries not to dwell on this question for too long.

It has been six months since he ended the relationship. This is his usual way: talks about merging our lives, how much he needs me; a night of passionate lovemaking; getting closer and deeper into the relationship, and then, two days later, creates a fight that doesn't make any sense; avoids the situation and won't return any of my calls; totally blows off the relationship as though it never existed; and discards me as a person and doesn't give me a chance to be heard. He left me feeling as though he has no value of me as a person and that I never mattered.

I am more upset with myself because I can't resist him. Two years ago, when Perry called for us to get back together after another one of his intimate flights, I told him no. But being lost to his adorable boyish charm and to all the right words that he said won me over.

I am not going to ride this roller-coaster again. He is the perfect boyfriend and gentleman when he has complete control of everything in his life and he feels secure with himself...until life throws him any unforeseen circumstances. He just can't handle more than one crisis at a time. The only thing he can control at that time is to push the relationship as far away as possible, with no regards to the pain and anguish that he inflicts. It is more devastating than anyone can imagine. It's the unconscious act from fear that causes such an evil deed to someone that is supposed to be their love.

This is why Dr. Fairchild has the fear that she, too, could be capable of some form of retaliation. To one whose heart has been emotionally played for a fool, deceit and betrayal does not equate love. She consciously refuses to become less of who she is and what she believes in.

Perry has become a part of her history, a collection of past experience that she is learning to respect and not to fear. This experience with Perry is a chapter in her life that she references as a book of knowledge and strength when the temptation arises to contact Perry, a source of direction and courage, which she applies both in her personal life and career. Their careers interact more than she cares to encounter, but she has learned to use Perry's expertise as a district attorney to her advantage and to keep their involvement on a professional basis.

Love is powerful and addicting. It can give life, but it can be deadly.

Dr. Fairchild and Libby arrive at the airport terminal. Dr. Fairchild removes her luggage from the trunk of the car.

"Thanks for all of your help, Libby. It means a lot to me. Sorry I wasn't much company on the way over; I just have a lot on my mind. I will call you when I am settled in my room," says Dr. Fairchild.

Dr. Fairchild walks briskly into the airport terminal, glad that she is the first one in line, and then checks in her baggage. She notices a husky built man with mannerisms of Columbo. He is there and obnoxious, moving from one side of the terminal to the other, watching her every move. She puts her e-tickets in her briefcase and heads towards Gate B2. Columbo continues to follow her, and when she picks up her pace, he moves more quickly, but keeping a distance as though to intimidate her and never allowing her out of his sight.

Don't panic, Bailey. There is probably a perfectly good explanation, a coincidence, she tries to convince herself.

The reassuring isn't working, especially when she backtracks towards him to get a better look at her stalker, and then the full impact of déjà vu hits her like a bolt of lightning. It's that sickening smell of the cigar odor that lingered in her condo for an eternity after her attack.

Dr. Fairchild tries to remember that night—his face, the smirk. It's all a fog. Then she remembers. *Why is he following me, and what does he want?*

Her heart is pounding loudly through her chest. She shows her ticket at the gate and pushes through to her seat, watching if he will board, anticipating where he will sit. She feels the uncontrollable urge to vomit. She feels weak and very vulnerable. In what seems to have taken forever, the flight attendant finally closes the door after the last passenger is seated. Relieved yet confused that Columbo didn't board, she questions who he is. And the reason he is following her haunted Dr. Fairchild throughout the flight.

The flight attendant asks Dr. Fairchild if she would like a snack or something to drink.

"A glass of chardonnay, please, and hold the snack." Dr. Fairchild is feeling nauseous and confused.

Dr. Fairchild, annoyed at herself, murmurs, "I should have brought my iPod. Maybe the music would have drowned out these continuous thoughts of Perry."

She realizes that this happens every time Perry calls her. The obsession and heartache starts all over again. His call to her this time was different. He left her a voice message on her cell phone. While listening to his words "I am dating Libby and planning to continue to see her," Dr. Fairchild's pulse flatlines almost to a point of passing out.

She lifts her empty glass towards the flight attendant, motioning for another chardonnay, saluting herself before sipping. She gives a big sigh and surrenders to her obsession back to the time when she and Perry had their first hike and being captured by his poetic charm. They hiked the seven-hundred-foot crest of Mount Royal, "the mountain," a panoramic view of the city in Canada. When they reached the top, Perry set a romantic moment, a French lunch for two that included smoked meat sandwiches and wine. She still feels his embracing arms dissolving her into his touch while she grows feverish with desire. They have given "the mountain" a whole new meaning.

There are many wonderful characteristics of Perry that kept Dr. Fairchild in love and tolerant of his avoidance to commitment. Their five years together had more unforgettable moments of love, travel, fun, and the times they were close enough to breathe the same air in silence. Just having each other in the same parameter sometimes was all they needed. Their harmony was contagious to those who were fortunate to indulge in their presence.

Each time Perry would get close in the relationship, he would run and push Dr. Fairchild away with no word, no explanation; they were just not available. His behavior sent her many mixed messages and would spiral her into devastation. The last flee was his last time to leave her heart shattered.

Dr. Fairchild has to grow strong from her wounds and keep Perry at bay.

Chapter Thirteen

Dr. Fairchild stares out the airplane window, fidgeting in the narrow seat. She is trying to place her butt in a comfortable position. Dr. Fairchild closes her eyes, reminiscing about the voice message from Perry. It is hard for her to grasp the fact that after five years of an on-again, off-again relationship, this is the final curtain for them. She is finally free from this emotional roller-coaster. Perry's words, "I am dating Libby," sent her heart in a down spin. She knew that someday this moment would come, but didn't anticipate that the pain would be so deep. A coating of burning fire smolders within the walls of her stomach.

Chapter Fourteen

While she replays his message in her mind, her heart grows sadder. If only it was someone different than Libby. Her chin quivers, holding back a flood of tears. *Libby is my best friend, my confidant, and my assistant.*

Dr. Fairchild bends down towards her wrist and wipes the tears from her cheek. She pulls a tissue from her purse, and, trying not to draw any attention to her blowing her nose, dabs the outer part of her nose and sniffles in.

Dr. Fairchild goes back to staring out the window. The wine is making her sleepy. The sheet of white clouds keep Dr. Fairchild hypnotized, unable to stop these thoughts of Perry. They are becoming an obsession. One of Perry's attributes is his poetic seductive charm that captures her whole being. It's an addiction that she knows she has to break away from. His continuous pattern is to capture her heart and then bolt from the relationship for months at a time, as though she had no value as a human being in his life.

While looking at her watch, she raises her right eyebrow and gives a half-crooked smile. Then she thinks to herself, *It's 7:30 p.m., and Libby will now be experiencing Perry's poetic seductive charm.*

Dr. Fairchild relives this moment in her mind and is devastated, knowing that, this time, it is becoming Libby's reality.

She's on time. It's 7:30 p.m. She drives her shiny blue and white convertible Shelby into Perry's circular driveway. He stands there erect and confident, pointing where he wants her to park the car. His dashing smile and big brown bedroom eyes awaits her. He opens the car door and holds out his right hand. The warmth of his hand makes her feel secure as he instantly pulls her towards his chest for an embrace that is too spectacular to define. The smell of his cologne stimulates her sensual side. He brushes her forehead with a stingy kiss and presses his hands on her back to steer her towards the catwalk that leads them to the Victorian French doors. He shifts his body behind her, puts his muscular arms around her shoulders, and ties a blindfold over her eyes.

"I have a surprise for you, and you can't peek," he says in a deep vibrating voice.

Perry opens the French doors and removes her shoes. Her bare feet feel the cold black marble slate. There's something soft and velvety touching the tip of her toes. Not knowing what lies beneath her feet, she shuffles forward and feels them fluttering around her ankles and feet. There's a familiar aroma. It's the smell of roses. Her curiosity is piqued.

"These must be rose petals," she mumbles to herself.

He guides her body by embracing his arm through hers to the staircase, tells her that she needs to step up, informs her that there are ten more stairs to climb, and that an ecstasy awaits her. The soft velvety rose petals caress her feet on every step to the top of the staircase. The trail of rose petals leads to his bedroom of ecstasy. There are rose petals everywhere and a new scent, vanilla. He gently lies her down on the bed, and, with his fingertips, pushes the blindfold onto her forehead and seductively tells her to open her eyes. Her eyes open to a ceiling of mirrors and the reflection of burning candles.

"Miss, are you all right?" the flight attendant asks.

Dr. Fairchild awakens from her journey and turns to the attendant.

"Yes, just reliving a life that is no longer mine!"

The flight attendant announces to the passengers that they should make sure all trays are fastened and seat belts are on for their landing.

Dr. Fairchild wipes the drool from the corner of her mouth, views herself in her compact mirror, and applies a minty flavored aloe vera lip balm, hoping that no one saw this embarrassing sight. She blames the wine and the puffy lip, a small reminder from her mystery attacker.

"Everyone, please remain in your seats until the plane has safely landed," announces the attendant.

Dr. Fairchild picks up her carry-on bag and heads towards the door of the plane. Cautiously, she looks over her shoulder and back to make sure no one is following her at the plane.

As she walks through the gate terminal, she hears someone calling her.

She dreads telling Korey why she has a black eye and a puffy lip. He will turn into an overbearing father with enough drama for the local playhouse.

I am already getting the start of a migraine. He will carry on into one of his endless lectures about me living alone.

"Bailey, you are walking as though someone is after you. Slow down and give your favorite pain-in-the-ass a big hug," shouted Korey. "What happened to you?"

Dr. Fairchild gives no reply, nods, and moves on.

"Come on, Bailey, this isn't like you to just look at me and nod to move on."

"Korey, calm down. It's not as bad as it looks."

She walks towards him and gives him a very embracing hug.

"I will tell you the details later, but not now. I have to get to the hotel and start putting my notes together for my meeting tomorrow with Dr. Kendall."

"I know. It's late."

"May I buy you a cup of coffee?"

"You are hiding something from me. We have worked too many years together, and I know when I am getting the brush off," says Korey.

"You are giving me a migraine. Please don't badger me. I am not changing my mind. Tomorrow we'll have lunch."

"My car is in the parking lot, would you like me to give you a lift to the hotel?" Korey asks.

"No, I will take the shuttle to the hotel. I am tired and need to be alone," replies Dr. Fairchild in a very depressed tone.

Korey orders a shuttle for Dr. Fairchild and gives the destination and a ten-dollar tip to the driver. This time, Korey keeps his distance from Dr. Fairchild. He loads her luggage on the shuttle, gives her a tap on her shoulder, and walks off towards the parking lot. In such a state of confusion about Dr. Fairchild's behavior, he walks with his head looking down at the ground and both hands in his pockets.

"How far is it to Caesar Atlantic City?" Dr. Fairchild asks the driver.

"Ten minutes," the driver replies.

Dr. Fairchild arrives at the hotel tired, hungry, and starting to feel the pain from her attack. She checks in.

"Good evening, are you checking in?"

"Yes, Dr. Bailey Fairchild." *No, I'm here for movie audition,* she thinks to herself sarcastically.

"Would you please schedule me a wake-up call for 6:00 a.m. tomorrow?" Dr. Fairchild requests.

"No problem!" assures the front desk clerk.

"Dr. Fairchild, you have two messages. One, from Dr. Kendall, hoping you can meet her an hour later at 4:00 p.m. Dr. Kendall paid your room. Here are your two keys, Room 1144. It's a suite with a Jacuzzi."

"You said I had two messages. What is the second one?" Dr. Fairchild asks.

"Yes, Dr. Fairchild. Second, from Libby, Mousey is okay, and she replaced the window and added bars. She said you would understand her cryptic message," replies the nervous clerk. "Enjoy your stay!"

"Thank you, I will."

Dr. Fairchild goes to the elevator, pushes the "up" arrow button, and waits for the doors to open. While she is waiting, she glances at herself in the mirror centered on the wall in between the two elevators. She is not impressed with the reflection. *I am too tired to give into my vanity tonight.*

She enters the elevator and pushes the number "11" button to her floor. She hesitates as she exits the elevator. There's a foreboding presence.

Is this paranoia? she questions this momentarily, and then pauses to locate the direction of her room by the numbered arrows stenciled on the wall opposite of the elevator. She steps into the corridor and walks left to her room. She slides the key card into the door and waits for the green light to signal her to pull down the handle.

Chapter Fifteen

Exhausted and hungry, she drops her luggage on the bed and sits at the desk to order room service. Dr. Fairchild calls Libby at the office as promised. There's no answer. She leaves a voice message, knowing Libby wouldn't get the message until the next morning.

I'm not ready to talk to her, not yet. These are Dr. Fairchild's thoughts before settling down for the night.

"This is Suite 1144, is it too late for room service?"

"No, the kitchen is open for two more hours."

After quickly reading the hotel menu, Dr. Fairchild orders dinner.

"I would like a glass of the Lockwood chardonnay, a well-done filet mignon, the end-piece, rice pilaf, and a Caesar salad with no croutons. Thanks."

"It will be there in forty-five minutes."

She thinks to herself, *Perfect, I have time for the Jacuzzi. Hopefully, between dinner and a Jacuzzi, this just might calm me down. I have a very intense few weeks ahead, and I need to be in more control of my emotions. I will have to apologize to Korey tomorrow for being such a bitch when he was trying to comfort me. The part of traveling that I hate the most is packing and unpacking. I will just take out what I need for tomorrow. I will deal with the rest later.*

Dr. Fairchild starts the Jacuzzi. She pulls her hair up in a comb. She removes her clothes and tosses them over the toilet seat. Carefully, she steps into the tub, anticipating the pressure of the jets strumming the hot water over her feet and up to her calves. She squats to feel the thrusting force all over her body. She stretches her body outward on her back, closes her eyes, and floats into an erotic ecstasy. The orgasm was interrupted before hitting its climax by a noise that startled her back to reality.

"Hello, who's there? May I help you?" Dr. Fairchild asks in a frightened voice.

She gets out of the tub. Water puddles form on the floor from her wet body, as she grabs a bathrobe hanging on the back of the door and quickly puts it on. She opens the bathroom door and quietly peeks to see if anyone is there. There's no one. She walks towards the bed. A sickening wave of terror welling up from her belly came when she saw a red lacy nightgown draped across the bed. She didn't put anything on the bed. Frightened, she calls the front desk.

"I am in Room 1144, did anyone asked for a key to my room?"

"No," says the front desk clerk.

Suddenly, there's a knock on the door. Dr. Fairchild trembles and her breath quickens.

"Who's there?" Dr. Fairchild cries out in a voice raw with terror.

"Room service, are you okay?"

She looks through the peephole and opens the door. She orders him to leave the tray on the floor and closes the door securing the safety lock. She questions herself on why she didn't secure the lock earlier.

Dr. Fairchild puts the red nightgown in an extra plastic garbage bag to have it analyzed by Dr. Kendall for any evidence of hair follicles or skin tissue. Paralyzed by the event, she sits on the bed and recoils in horror, just trying to get through the night.

The early morning is getting the best of Dr. Fairchild; she doesn't sleep and is only in a state of reverie.

Chapter Sixteen

Dr. Fairchild is startled out of her daydream by the phone ringing. She feels as though she just closed her eyes, wishing she could pull the covers over her head and sleep for an eternity.

"Hello!" Dr. Fairchild answers the phone with a groggy voice.

"Good morning, Dr. Fairchild, this is your wake-up call!" says the front desk clerk with an annoying perky voice.

"Thank you!" replies Dr. Fairchild graciously.

While she hangs up the receiver, she thinks to herself, *It's too early for such perkiness. I need a café au lait to get me started this morning.*

She rolls herself out of bed, contemplating what to wear for the day, keeping in mind that she will spend most of the day in a cold coroner's office.

There is a knock at the door. Dr. Fairchild looks through the peephole, and it is Korey Scott.

"Good Morning, Bailey. I have something for you!" Korey says in a perky voice.

"Has everyone overdosed on perky pills?"

"Did you wake up on the wrong side of the bed?" Korey asks.

"I brought you a café au lait. I called the front desk to see if room service would deliver you a café au lait; not on the menu. I know how you are in the morning, and, after seeing you last night, I thought this might perk you up!" states Korey.

"We are scheduled to have lunch today. You could have waited until then," replies Dr. Fairchild.

"I don't mean to be rude, but I have to jump in the shower and go over these notes before our lunch meeting and my appointment with Dr. Kendall at 4:00 p.m."

Korey starts to walk away from the door, feeling another one of Dr. Fairchild's brush-offs. It's not that he wanted more than to deliver the coffee, but he hopes that Dr. Fairchild would have been a little less professional.

"Korey, thank you for being so thoughtful. You are such a dear friend," Dr. Fairchild responds in an appreciative tone.

Dr. Fairchild shuts the door. Before Korey walks down the corridor, he touches the door and thinks to himself, *I am falling in love with you, Bailey.*

Korey has always been attracted to Dr. Fairchild, but who wouldn't? She is beautiful, intelligent, mature, successful, and very sexy. He also knows his competition, Perry Sinclair, who has Dr. Fairchild's heart and probably always will. Knowing this is the reason why Korey won't tell Dr. Fairchild his true feelings for her.

Chapter Seventeen

Dr. Fairchild puts the final touches to her hair and makeup. She tucks in her white Victorian silk blouse into her teal suede pants and ties a scarf around her waist that drapes down the right side of her hip to the middle of her thigh. The scarf background is white, with mauve and lavender roses intricately weaving through teal threads, creating a pattern of delicate leaves. Her long, wavy, thick auburn hair accentuates the outfit, making her absolutely stunning. Dr. Fairchild primps a few times in the mirror, impressed with how she looks.

If it's cold in the coroner's office, I will just have to wear one of those white lab coats. Dr. Fairchild runs this thought briefly through her mind. She's hoping to make an unforgettable impression to Korey at lunch. She grabs her briefcase that contains the ME notes and the plastic bag with the red nightgown.

Dr. Fairchild arrives at Scannicchio's Italian Restaurant on California Avenue. She is very nervous, there are butterflies in her stomach.

Come on, Bailey. It is only Korey you are having lunch with, not a high school prom date. These are her thoughts as she enters the restaurant.

Korey greets Dr. Fairchild at the door with his gorgeous radiant smile.

"Bailey, you are absolutely stunning," says Korey.

"Thank you, you are quite handsome yourself," Dr. Fairchild retorts.

"The restaurant isn't exactly what I had in mind. The ambiance is cozy and a little crowded. The food is the best Italian in Atlantic City that I was told by the taxi driver. It was the location. Being so close to your hotel and the coroner's office, I thought this would be the best for your time schedule," says Korey.

"It is lovely. You are always so very thoughtful. The music is very romantic," says Dr. Fairchild.

"The driver said most of their desserts are baked on the premises. And he highly recommends the rum cake, ricotta cheesecake, or the cannoli. All are delectable."

"Would you like a glass of wine?" Korey asks.

"Yes, only a glass. I have to meet the ME after lunch," Dr. Fairchild answers with a smile.

The waiter comes to their table. He tells them the specials of the day and wine suggestions.

"We would like to start with a glass of La Villa Inglewood White Zinfandel," says Korey.

"Are you ready to order?" the waiter asks.

"Yes, the lady would like the Alla Scannicchio salad, and I would like the Caesar, and we both want the shrimp parmigiana."

Their wine is served.

"I would like to toast to you, Bailey. To a beautiful friend and coworker whom I am very grateful to have in my life."

They toast and as Dr. Fairchild sips her wine, she flirtatiously winks at Korey. This is the first time in the years of them working together that Dr. Fairchild is seeing Korey in a different light. She wonders if it is the wine making her very relaxed, or if these feelings have been there and she have suppressed them because of her questionable love towards Perry.

"Okay, you promised me that you would tell what happened to you prior to your coming to New Jersey. I did talk to Libby and she didn't say much, only that it is very dangerous," Korey reminds Dr. Fairchild.

"My condo was broken into, and I was attacked. The intruder took my laptop and rummaged through some of my notes on my desk," Dr. Fairchild replies.

"Bailey, I am not buying that this is all that happened. I am sure there is a lot more to this. You have been extremely preoccupied and jumpy. I saw your face...your puffy lip and black eye," says Korey.

"This all happened right after I was called by Dr. Kendall to go over the autopsy of the body that was found in the cranberry bogs. I feel this was a warning. This must be a very big case to have two big thugs attack me, and the mayor putting the pressure on Dr. Kendall to expedite the autopsy," Dr. Fairchild explains.

"Bailey, you know that I am here for you. Is there anything that I can do?" Korey asks.

"I need you to investigate everyone involved in this murder. I want you to start with Atlantic City Mayor Vince Sterlino. Find out if or what his connection maybe to this victim. The more information you can get to me the better. My intuition is telling me that if we don't find leads sooner than later to this heinous crime, there will be more victims."

Chapter Eighteen

Dr. Fairchild and Korey enjoy their wine and meal. The waiter asks them if they had room for dessert. Both decides to pass on dessert, but would come back another time for dessert and coffee. Dr. Fairchild flips open her elegant diamond watch cover and notices that the time is 3:40 p.m. In a hurried gesture, she pushes away from the table.

"Oh, I've got to go. I have to meet Dr. Kendall at 4:00 p.m. Korey, thank you for the wonderful lunch, and I enjoyed our conversation. It was nice that you didn't harp about me living alone."

"Would it have made a difference?" Korey asks.

"No, I don't think so."

Korey walks Dr. Fairchild five blocks to the coroner's office, opens the door to the lobby, looks around to make sure no one is viewing them, and gently pulls her towards him. He graciously pressed against her pelvis area, holds her securely close to him, and seals the moment with a kiss on her forehead. She feels her heart pounding, her pulse pumping with anticipation of how far Korey will go. She closes her eyes and, for a moment, feels weak and safe at the same time.

Korey moves his lips to her ear and whispers softly, "I will call you later."

He gallantly walks away.

Dr. Fairchild takes three deep breaths and fidgets her clothes back in place. She goes into the ladies room to freshen up before meeting with Dr. Kendall. She brushes her auburn mane and applies a fresh coat of lipstick. She smiles as she pushes the glossy stick along her lips and stares at herself in the mirror in pure satisfaction of the intense moment with Korey.

Chapter Nineteen

Dr. Fairchild decides to walk up the four flights of stairs to the coroner's office, feeling as though she could float her way up after her rendezvous with Korey. She pushes open the double stainless steel doors into the Medical Examiner's lab. Dr. Fairchild enters the lab with confidence and with an attitude to get this case closed. She grabs a white heavy cotton lab coat from the coat rack and drapes the coat over her shoulders. She fidgets for a few seconds in getting her arms into the sleeves, snaps the top two buttons together, and proceeds to the table where Dr. Kendall was recording the autopsy. She opens her briefcase and pulls out the notes and the plastic bag with the red nightgown.

"Hello, Dr. Fairchild, thank you for coming. I really do appreciate your expertise," says Dr. Kendall.

"Hello, Dr. Kendall, I need you to run some DNA test on this nightgown. It was a gift that was left for me last night. It was meticulously draped over the bed in my hotel room. I was in the bathtub when I heard a noise, and, when I went in the room, no one was there. The front desk said they didn't give a key to my room to anyone," Dr. Fairchild explains.

"Is that what happened to you? You look awful," says Dr. Kendall.

"No. I had a surprise attacker at my condo. This happened right after I spoke with Korey requesting my forensic expertise to assist in solving the murder of your Jane Doe. I feel that the attack was more of a warning. I could have been hurt a lot worse," says Dr. Fairchild.

"Warning about what?" Dr. Kendall asks.

"Whoever is behind this or involved doesn't want this case solved or be in the media. That is why I asked Korey to question the mayor and to find out if the mayor has any connection to Jane Doe," says Dr. Fairchild. "Have you done anymore of the autopsy?" she asks.

"Before I answer that question, please call me Katherine. And, yes, I did. I discovered that the red blotches on the abdomen were from the *Apoidea* family—bee stings. There were hundreds of stingers from the honeybee, bumblebee, and wasp," says Dr. Kendall. "The cranberry bogs are located in southern New Jersey, and, in the summer, it is very hot. There would be swarms of bees gathering to pollinate."

"That makes sense. This gives us a more definitive time of death—sometime in September," Dr. Fairchild speculates.

"Dr. Fairchild, you have an interesting first name."

"Please, call me Bailey. Bailey was my grandmother's maiden name and Fairchild is my grandfather's surname. Both my grandparents are descendants from Ireland. They were the first generation born in America. Annabel Bailey met Paddy Fairchild in New York in a subway. It was love at first sight for Paddy. Soon, thereafter, they were married and moved to Fort Morgan, Alabama where my grandfather was stationed in the military.

"I am very close to my grandfather. Paddy raised me from the time I was three years old, alone. He is the most loving and tender man I have ever known. My mother died during birth, and I was left to my grandparents. They adopted me, and just a few months before I turned three, my grandmother died from cancer," says Dr. Fairchild.

"What happened to your father?" Dr. Kendall questions.

"That was a subject that was never discussed. All I know is that my father left in a hurry, and we have never heard from him.

"Katherine, I would like to examine the body and review your notes. I have my colleague, Korey Scott, questioning the mayor to see if he can conclude why the mayor is in such a hurry to close this case. I have a feeling there is more to this, and we are just beginning to scratch the surface of something quite nasty," remarks Dr. Fairchild.

Chapter Twenty

Dr. Fairchild proceeds with the examination and reviews Dr. Kendall's notes. She compares the notes step by step to the body. Dr. Kendall places the transparencies that have written formulas on the slide projector for better viewing. She also starts the DNA testing on the nightgown.

After hours into the examination, Dr. Fairchild realizes that the coroner's lab is cold, extremely quiet, and very eerie. Something, a sense, puts a chill up her spine. She starts to feel anxious. And then there is a familiar aroma, the scent of a sweet stale cigar. The sound of scuffling shoes in the hallway adjacent to the lab is magnified by someone trying to control the noise, trying not to be heard. Dr. Fairchild points her finger at the tape recorder, motioning Dr. Kendall to turn it on. Dr. Kendall presses the RECORD button, as a shadow of a man crouches across the front of the doors, hoping not to be seen.

"I know there is someone there. What do you want?" Dr. Fairchild shouts.

There is no response. In a flash of a moment, the lab doors are pushed open abruptly and gunshots are fired. Dr. Fairchild pushes Dr. Kendall to the floor. Then she picks up the lab chair and swings it into the air, breaking the hanging light fixture. Now, there is darkness. The gunshots have stopped. There is no sound and no gunman. There is only the smell of the smoke from the gunshots and the sweet stale stench of a cigar.

"Dr. Kendall, are you okay?" Dr. Fairchild asks.

No response.

"Katherine," Dr. Fairchild calls out.

"I am okay. Just a little dazed when you threw me on the floor. I hit my head on the cabinet," replies a scared Dr. Kendall. "What happened? And what is that...God, awful smell?"

"I believe that was the same man who attacked me the first time. As I was passing out, the one thing that I remembered about him is that he was smoking a cigar. That awful smell is the sweet stale cigar that he was smoking then and now. I should have told you the details. I just didn't think he would be back so soon.

"What doesn't make sense about this attack is he could have shot us both. The gunshots were fired randomly in the lab and not at us," Dr. Fairchild's voice quivers with fear and anger.

Both are startled when Dr. Fairchild's cell phone vibrates across the floor. She reads the caller ID, and it's Paddy.

"Hello," Dr. Fairchild answers with a shaken voice.

"How's my Snowbird? I was hoping that you might be able to come and visit me soon. I have your birthday present, and it's been months since I have seen you.

"You sound a little upset, are you okay?" Paddy asks with concern in a very strong Irish accent.

"I am okay. I have been very busy on a new case, and there are a lot of forensic details that need some clarification. I'm just a little tired.

"I will have to call you back tomorrow, Paddy. I will check my schedule to see when I will be able to come for a visit."

"I love you, Snowbird. Take care!" says Paddy.

"I will call you later," Dr. Fairchild presses the END button on the cell and disengages from Paddy.

Paddy hangs up, feeling there is more to Dr. Fairchild's tone in her voice than just being busy and a little tired. He goes back to assisting a customer in his bait and bicycle shop on Dauphin Island.

Chapter Twenty-One

"Sorry about that. Talk about poor timing. I am going to call Korey and have him meet us here," says Dr. Fairchild.

"Don't you think we should call the police?" Dr. Kendall asks.

"No!"

"Why not?"

"It's getting too dangerous. I would like to wait and see what information Korey has compiled. If the mayor is part of this, he will probably own the police department and this will flagged them that we are suspicious. Right now, they are not sure of what we know, except for the butchered body. I want to get more proof and not risk the chance to nail these assholes to the wall," replies Dr. Fairchild.

"I see what you are saying, Bailey. My God, how are you getting through this? This was your second attack, and they seem to be escalating and becoming more dangerous," Dr. Kendall asks.

"My faith is in God. I know this career is what he planned for me, and he has protected and guided me through it all. I love what I do. There is a rush that flows throughout my body, a high, an addiction to solve the crime and give justice for the victims.

"Katherine, your notes indicate that Jane Doe had breast implants. I examined the tissues and the surgery area of the breast. The plastic surgeon who performed the implants was meticulous and has a unique style of cutting. Every plastic surgeon has their own style; it's their signature. Each cut is unique and not the same as any other surgeon. I spliced a thin lining of the gel and discovered numbers. I want you to see under the microscope the numbers that are engraved in the lining. These numbers are like serial numbers used to identify their type, style, and what pharmaceutical company produced them," Dr. Fairchild points out.

Dr. Fairchild begins to review the autopsy results with Dr. Kendall.

Dr. Kendall pulls her chair to the table, moves the slide with the specimen in position, and views Dr. Fairchild's findings.

"Impressive, how did I miss this?" Dr. Kendall asks.

"I have done many autopsies on breast implants, and, unless you are aware of what to look for, it's easy to miss," Dr. Fairchild replies.

"Now, you know why you are needed and highly respected." Dr. Kendall chuckled.

"I am going to call Korey and see what he has unfolded with the mayor. We will need someone from your lab to investigate these numbers. As soon as we locate where these implants were made and where they were sold, this will then lead us to the hospital, the surgeon, and the identity of Jane Doe," says Dr. Fairchild.

"I will have my assistant, Lora Michele, do the research. She is studying to be a criminologist and is amazing in forensics. She works for me part time. Lora is incredibly efficient and extremely intelligent. I will call her tomorrow.

"It's eight o'clock. Let's call it a night. We can meet back tomorrow at 9:00 a.m.," says Dr. Kendall in an exhausting tone.

"Hello, security, this is Dr. Kendall. Please have my car brought to the front of the building. I will be down in ten minutes. Thank you."

"Tomorrow it is. Good night," Dr. Fairchild replies.

"Good night!"

Chapter Twenty-Two

They leave the crime scene intact, lock the lab doors, and, as they walk down the corridor, Korey appears at the end of the hall. Dr. Kendall takes the elevator down to the lobby.

"I was just going to call you to see how it went with the mayor and asked for a ride back to the hotel."

"Well, interesting you should ask. I went to the mayor's office and asked the receptionist if Vince Sterlino was in. She said no and asked if I had an appointment with the mayor. Just when I was going to answer her, I heard a door in his office slam. Without any hesitation, I forced myself through his main doors and entered in the office. And this is what I retrieved," says Korey.

Korey dangles a plastic bag in the air with his right hand. Inside the plastic bag were pieces of a burnt cigar, cigar butt, and ashes.

"The mayor must have just exited the back door when I entered. The cigar was just put out, it was smoldering," Korey says.

"Excellent! Tomorrow we will have Dr. Kendall's staff run DNA test. Interesting, though, if this matches the cigar ashes in the ME lab, this person could be Columbo, the man who attacked me in Canada, and possibly, the same man at ME lab," says Dr. Fairchild.

"What ashes in the ME lab? What happened?" Korey asks.

"Around six o'clock, Dr. Kendall and I heard someone in the corridor, and then he came bursting through the lab doors with open gunfire. Thank God we weren't hurt."

"Bailey, if the cigar matches, this means that it was the mayor who was in your condo, and either did the attack or was an accomplice," says Korey.

"Maybe. Why would a mayor waste his time and taxpayer's money following me?" Dr. Fairchild replies with concern in her voice.

"Korey, what time were you at the mayor's office?"

"I was in his lobby about 4:30 p.m., and I busted my way in around 5:00 p.m. I know the time because the receptionist started locking up her area asking everyone to leave because they close at 5:00 p.m. When I approached her to go into Mr. Sterlino's office is when I heard a door slam from inside his office."

"How far would you say it is from the mayor's office to the coroner's?" Dr. Fairchild asks.

"I would say at least forty-five minutes by the time he walks to his car and snails his way through the commute traffic," replies Korey.

"Would it be possible for you to trail the mayor?" Dr. Fairchild asks.

"I will start first thing tomorrow," replies Korey.

"I haven't called the police on any of the attacks. My intuition is telling me to get more facts before we pursue with the police. If the person or persons involved are as evil and devious as they seem, we need to be extremely thorough and cautious on this case. I don't want them to get away with this due to a lack of evidence or technicalities," says Dr. Fairchild. "Thank you for dropping me off. Call me tomorrow. Good night."

"I'll call you soon," Korey assuredly states.

Chapter Twenty-Three

Dr. Fairchild smiles at the valet attendant as she walks by towards the entrance of the hotel.

"Good evening, Miss!" says the valet attendant to Dr. Fairchild with a smile.

"Good evening."

She continues with her mission through the revolving doors and heads towards the front desk.

"Hello, I am Dr. Fairchild. I am in Room 1144. Do I have any messages?"

"Good evening. Yes, you have one message!" replies the front desk clerk.

"Thank you. And please set a wake-up call for tomorrow at 6:00 a.m."

The clerk nods his head in gesture as an acknowledgement of her request and proceeds to program the computer phone accordingly.

Dr. Fairchild walks to the elevators that are directly across from the front desk, presses the "up" button, and waits for her destination to her floor. While waiting, Dr. Fairchild opens the sealed envelope to read her message. Her focus on the message is interrupted when the elevator doors open. She enters cautiously, scoping the surroundings for any unwanted passengers. Dr. Fairchild sighs with relief that she is alone and reaches to push button "11" for her floor. A leather glove presses the button that enables her to succeed. A man swings his body in front of Dr. Fairchild to position himself with the glove. The doors close. Dr. Fairchild backs herself into the corner, trying not to show the fear that is racing through her veins, anticipating his next move.

The elevator stops at the eleventh floor. Doors open, and Dr. Fairchild waits for the short bald man wearing a raincoat to exit. He smiles at her and walks to the left of the elevator, heading down the hall in the same direction of her room. In fear that he could be her attacker, she slows down her pace, not letting him out of her sight. He passes her room to the end of the hall, fumbles for his key card, and enters. Dr. Fairchild quickly runs to her room, slides her key card, pulls the handle, and enters, shutting the door abruptly. She bolts and pulls the security locks, presses the light switch, and proceeds to the phone to call the front desk.

"Hello, this is Dr. Fairchild in Room 1144. Would you please tell me who is in the room down the hall next to the EXIT sign? The gentleman looks like a colleague of mine, and I wanted to call and see if he was available for breakfast in the morning!" a scared Dr. Fairchild asks.

"Dr. Fairchild, according to the hotel policy, we are not allowed to give out any names of the hotel guests. I can tell you that he is attending the New Jersey Writer's Conference that is being held at the hotel," replies the front desk.

"Should I leave him a message from you?"

"Thank you. No, that won't be necessary. You have been extremely helpful."

Well, Bailey, this case really has you extremely paranoid. Maybe a hot bath with cucumber melon bubbles will soak out this tension. I need a good night's sleep.

Chapter Twenty-Four

The hot bubble bath tranquilizes Dr. Fairchild's whole body, allaying her fears temporarily. Then the hot bath suddenly betrays her. Becoming cold, it abruptly awakens her from a deep sleep. She pulls the plug and watches the water drain before standing up and reaching for a towel; she pats herself dry. Even though her body is cold, Dr. Fairchild slowly pulls her pink silky nightgown over her head, and, down past her shoulders, she lets the hem graciously flow to her knees. So tired, she ignores her vanity, avoids the bathroom mirror, and shuffles her body to the bed. She gently pulls the comforter back, allowing her enough room to snuggle under the covers and instantly falls asleep.

Chapter Twenty-Five

The phone rings in Dr. Fairchild's room. She fumbles for the phone and looks at the clock. It is 5:30 a.m. It's Dr. Kendall.

"Bailey, I need you in the lab immediately. I couldn't sleep and wanted to do more on the breast implants. I've been stirring all night. Be prepared when you walk in the lab. It's shocking," Dr. Kendall screams rapidly. Her words that electrifies fear is heard through the phone.

Before Dr. Fairchild could respond, Dr. Kendall hangs up. Dr. Fairchild dashes out of bed and throws on a pair of jeans and a lacy blouse. She washes her face, brushes her teeth, and throws her hair in a ponytail. She calls the front desk requesting a taxi. While entering the taxi, Dr. Fairchild calls Korey and requests that he meets them at the lab. She continues to primp herself.

Dr. Fairchild approaches the lab and senses that there is something extremely eerie while entering through the metal doors. There is no stale cigar smell, only the scent of bleach. There are no bullet shells or broken glass on the floor. The hanging lamp is very still and complete; no evidence of having any broken glass. The lab room is immaculate. There are no cigar ashes or any trace of yesterday's gunshot spree ever existed.

Dr. Kendall hands Dr. Fairchild a cup of coffee.

"When I came to the lab, the doors were unhinged. I couldn't believe what I was envisioning—a very well-cleaned lab. There isn't any evidence of what happened last evening," says Dr. Kendall.

"Did they get the breast implant tissues?" Dr. Fairchild asks.

"No. Last night, I immediately went back to the lab and put all the autopsy tissues and research material in a locked cooler. I am the only one who knows the combination. My staff doesn't use this cooler. It's used for my autopsies. I decided on this after what has been happening to you through this whole investigation. It's probably a little over the top, but yesterday's encounter made me a little nervous," replies Dr. Kendall.

"I think it was ingenious. Obviously, we are getting close. Let's start on the autopsy and the breast implants. Call your assistant and see what her status is on the serial numbers. This is a priority. All staff members need to focus on this case." Dr. Fairchild meant business. Her gruff tone made it convincing.

"There is a problem. The nightgown is gone. I didn't get a chance to start the DNA," Dr. Kendall walks to the window and stands erect, displaying a withering stare of disgust.

"It's okay. The nightgown was simply a deployment in hopes that I would be frightened enough to quit," Dr. Fairchild states confidently.

Chapter Twenty-Six

Korey enters the lab. He has an expression of dismay on his face as he views the room.

"This is a joke. Where's the evidence that was left here last night?" Korey asks in disbelief.

"This room looked like a bomb went off."

"We don't know. This is what I found when I walked in about a half hour ago. It's unbelievable. Everything is cleaned up and replaced. I put the tissues and research material in a locked cooler. I came back after we left last night. I had bad vibes from the incident," replies Dr. Kendall.

"Korey, I need you to do a thorough research on the mayor, his family background, anything and everything. We are going to hit the autopsy aggressively," Dr. Fairchild states.

"I plan to be at the Atlantic City library as soon as they open. I want to see if there are any newspaper articles regarding the mayor," Korey states confidently. "I will see you later."

"Bailey, I received the status information on the breast implants from my assistant. The serial numbers are from PLASCO-bh Manufacturing. They supply only to the plastic surgeons in Beverly Hills. The 'bh' symbolizes for that market. What is astonishing these particular implants are designed only for the Beverly Hills Medical Research Center, and only a selected few surgeons use these because they are extremely expensive. One breast implant—depending on the size and type—could start at a mere $8,000. Our Jane Doe, according to her serial numbers, had the works which cost her $10,000 per breast implant," explained Dr. Kendall.

"Interesting. This makes sense why all that was left was her torso. And...was Lora Michele able to locate the surgeon?" Dr. Fairchild asks.

"No. She is still working on that. Our Jane Doe is someone very rich or has a very wealthy husband or boyfriend," replies Dr. Kendall.

Dr. Fairchild calls Korey and leaves a message on his cell. She asks him to return her call with the status on any newspaper articles or background information on the mayor.

Korey enters the computer area of the library and downloads all the newspaper articles on Vince Sterlino, mayor of Atlantic City, New Jersey for a period of ten years. There are quite a few articles on the mayor commending him on his community works and projects for the schools and churches, but there is one article that stood out and caught Korey's attention. It is the mayor's only front page article. The article is printed on the fifteenth of December. It is inviting the community to a New Year's Ball with a picture of the mayor and his sister, Margaret Sterlino Huntington. She is the widow of the late Dr. Marcus Huntington Sr., a highly respected breast cancer surgeon. Their son, Dr. Marcus Huntington Jr., is a plastic surgeon in Beverly Hills. This gala event is a fundraiser for breast cancer research in memory of Dr. Marcus Huntington Sr.

Korey prints a copy of the article and leaves the library. Amazed at what he found, he returns Dr. Fairchild's call with the new information.

Chapter Twenty-Seven

Dr. Fairchild collects her messages from the front desk clerk and reads the one that she was surprised to receive.

Dear Bailey,
*   This isn't urgent. Please call when you have some time to talk.*
*   Perry Sinclair*

Just as Dr. Fairchild is picking up the phone to call Perry, Korey calls. Korey's name scrolls across Dr. Fairchild's caller ID. Dr. Fairchild decides to let Korey's call go into voicemail.

Chapter Twenty-Eight

This is Libby's opportunity to enact her obsession with Dr. Fairchild's life. It isn't enough to have an affair with Perry, she wants to be Dr. Fairchild. Libby anticipates her moments of pleasure at Dr. Fairchild's condo. Having to watch Mousey is the perfect excuse to wear Dr. Fairchild's clothes, drive her turquoise 1955 T-Bird, and weave Perry into her web of deception.

Libby is plotting her next rendezvous with Perry. This evening's event is well staged. The candlelit dinner is accompanied by classical music. She is even wearing Dr. Fairchild's clothes. What makes the evening more appetizing for Libby is that she knows she is doing all of this in Dr. Fairchild's condo with Perry.

Libby shuffles through Dr. Fairchild's clothes from hanger to hanger, trying to decide what outfit to wear that will entice Perry. Her accomplice has been found, a beautiful black sequins negligee. The black satin marabou heels completes the attire for the evening.

The obsession with Dr. Fairchild comes through Libby; the transformation is uncanny.

Libby stares at herself in the mirror, admiring the art that she has created.

"Unbelievable," she mutters under her breath.

Impressed with the stunning results, her hair, makeup, and clothes reflect Dr. Fairchild almost to perfection. Libby primps one more time, drooling over herself.

She prances down the stairs to answer the door in hopes that Perry will be enthralled, as she is, over her transformation.

"Wow, you are absolutely ravishing."

"What's the occasion?" Perry inquires.

"No occasion. It's simply to be irresistible in hopes to stimulate your appetite before dinner," Libby states flirtatiously.

"Do you find me as attractive as Bailey?" she asks.

Libby places the olives in Perry's martini glass and hands the drink to him.

"Honestly, at first, I thought you were Bailey. Why the theatrics?" An edge of impatience was creeping in Perry's voice.

"Why not? I know how you feel about Bailey, and I thought this might get you closer to me," Libby responds defensively.

"You are not Bailey!"

Perry isn't impressed with Libby's insane obsession to look and act like Dr. Fairchild. He finishes his martini and decides to leave before dinner. This whole escapade from Libby was unnerving.

Libby is beside herself. Perry's response isn't what she has anticipated. He isn't enticed or impressed by her appearance.

"Libby, I don't know what you were thinking or trying to accomplish, but I am appalled with your obsession over Bailey. We are through."

Perry leaves the condo in such shock and disbelief, confused over his misjudgment of her character, her obsession. Perry questions his feelings and attraction for Libby. Is it just his sexual appetite being satisfied or is there a deeper hidden agenda?

Could it possibly be a form of retaliation towards Dr. Fairchild for not taking him back into her life once again?

Perry pulls out of the driveway and heads for home. In less than two minutes on the road, his cell phone rings. It's Libby's number scrolling across the view pane. He lets it go into voicemail. She calls again and he repeats his last response. He doesn't want to engage in any of Libby's drama or meaningless conversation.

Perry's drive home is less than relaxing. The pressure in his chest is heavier and isn't subsiding. The more he thinks about Libby's charade, the more the pressure increases and the pain intensifies. He is sure he is having a heart attack.

The journey from his carport to the front door would normally be a hop, skip, and a jump. But Perry could barely get from the car to the walk path without feeling at any moment that he is going to pass out.

He makes it through the door to the kitchen, grabs a cold beer, and drops on the couch. Perry's eyes close. His mind wanders into the web of deceit, infidelity, and regret. The pain continues. Perry turns the cell phone off.

To avoid the chance of Libby calling his office, Perry decides to listen to his voicemail. He hears a thread of many disturbing messages.

Libby, scorned by Perry's rejection, is clearly understood in her message. Perry is still trying to put the evening's charade and phone message into perspective. He decides not to return her call as she demanded.

He is having a hard time believing Libby's message that *she's pregnant*.

Chapter Twenty-Nine

"Oh no, Mousey!"

"What is this mess?" screeches Libby.

Mousey leaves evidence on the floor that what she ate disagreed with her pedigree tummy. Mousey has an allergic reaction from the dinner that was made for Perry the evening before. The shrimp cocktail is a dish that isn't one of her regular morsels. Mousey continuous to vomit. Panic-stricken, Libby calls the veterinarian for advice. Libby grabs Mousey and puts her in a cat carrier. Their journey to the vet isn't on her agenda. After a long ordeal of tests, shots, and a cat hissing and biting, the vet suggests that Mousey stay overnight for observation. Libby decides not to attempt to reach Dr. Fairchild and took Mousey home. She puts Mousey in the carrier and abruptly walks out. She straps the carrier into the passenger front seat of the T-Bird.

There is a very strong odor. Mousey is getting sick. The extremely hot day is intensifying the aroma. Libby zips back the top of the carrier, exposing the mesh lining for ventilation. Libby knows that if Dr. Fairchild finds out she has been driving her car, let alone her cat vomiting all over the front seat, she will go ballistic.

Libby decides to take the T-Bird to the car wash. She pulls the car to the entrance.

"Good afternoon, Dr. Fairchild."

"Is it the works today?" the attendant asks. He is confident it is Dr. Fairchild. He knows the license plate: PADDY.

Libby tips the yellow picture hat to block part of her left side and nods yes. Her facial expression displays her satisfaction over her successful accomplishment in deceiving the attendant. He motions her to move the car towards the pulley. The car jolts upward and pulls towards the water sprayer brushes, with soap suds swishing around the car. There was a second jolt, this time, a little harder. The jets start to increase in speed, and more suds covered the car as it stops. There's a violent bang on the driver's window. Scared, confused, and unable to see through the suds, she rolls down the window midway, in hopes of being helped.

Abruptly, a hand grabs the back of her hair and pushes her head violently down onto the steering wheel over and over again. Libby screams for help and fights with all her strength. She grabs its hands, trying to fight the assailant in the midst of the slippery suds. The more she fights, the harder the assailant thrashes her head against the steering wheel until it finally strangles the last breath of air out of Libby.

Mousey escapes from the carrier, frightened. She claws and scratches Libby's face and arms as she tries to gain a secure place for leverage to go out a partially opened window. She found a passage to her freedom.

Libby is less fortunate. Her body slumps over to her right side, motionless. Her face is bloody from Mousey's scratches, and it has been disfigured from the powerful blows onto the steering wheel. The assailant's mission is a success.

The car moves to the exit of the ramp. No one is in sight.

Chapter Thirty

Commissioner Gregory LaFleur from the Ontario Provincial Police records the grueling details of a homicide. It is heartbreaking and hard to believe that the eminent Dr. Bailey Fairchild was found murdered. The district attorney, Perry Sinclair, is notified of this tragedy. Their professional and personal relationship is known throughout Canada and highly respected.

Perry arrives at the car wash, dismayed and surprised by the call. He just spoke to Dr. Fairchild that morning. He called her at her hotel in Atlantic City, New Jersey. Mystified and preoccupied, Perry is beckoned back to reality by an intense but caring display of a rapid flow of emotional words.

"Mr. Sinclair, thanks for coming. I need you to identify the deceased. Everyone knows Dr. Fairchild, but I need an official confirmation for our records," states Commissioner LaFleur, sheepishly wiping tears away. His strong French accent makes his words hard to understand. "Prepare yourself, it isn't a pretty sight."

Perry gulps and tries to bring moisture to his throat, still confused and hoping this is a nasty mistake of identity.

Perry steps into puddles of water and suds, which follows the path that leads to the car. His heart starts pulsating; he feels the pounding down to his feet. The pounding intensifies as he gets closer and closer to the partially visible car. Perry doesn't want to believe what he sees. The glimpse of the T-Bird hood momentarily stops his breathing. His chest pains have been flaming and a panic attack has erupted.

God, please let there be another explanation. Don't let it be Bailey. Perry plays these thoughts over and over in his mind as he approaches the car.

He pauses and leans into the car window. At a single glance, he knows it is Libby. He is relieved that it isn't Dr. Fairchild, but he is saddened for Libby.

"Commissioner, this isn't Dr. Fairchild," Perry squeals, trying not to sound excitable.

"Are you sure?" asks the commissioner.

"Yes. It's Libby Grayson, Bailey's personal assistant. Bailey is back East in New Jersey. She is working on a murder case. I talked to her this morning."

"Why didn't you say something when you arrived?"

"I almost did until I saw her car, and, for a brief moment, I wasn't sure what to believe. I apologize that I didn't say something. I just had to be sure. It must be the district attorney mentality. We work on facts, no doubts," states Perry.

"Do you know Libby Grayson? Or should I ask, how well do you know Ms. Grayson?" the commissioner inquires suspiciously.

Perry is sensing the suspicion in the commissioner's voice and realizes that the only answer is the truthful answer.

"Ms. Grayson was my girlfriend. We dated for almost six months, and we broke up two nights ago. There were some very peculiar scenarios that Libby was betraying, and I didn't want to be part of it," Perry states sheepishly.

"That puts you with Ms. Grayson Wednesday evening. You stated there were some very peculiar scenarios. Would you please explain these to me?"

"Libby invited me to have dinner at Bailey's condo. As I mentioned earlier, Libby is Bailey's personal assistant and she also house manages and watches her cat. When I arrived, she opened the door wearing Bailey's clothes, perfume. She made my favorite dish that Bailey made for me. She wore her hair and makeup like Bailey. At first, I thought she was Bailey. Her obsession with Bailey was quite unnerving," explains Perry.

"How long were you there?"

"Not for very long. I finished my martini and left."

"You didn't answer my question. How long were you there?"

"No more than twenty minutes. Enough time to be sickened and to feel repulsive. I had to get out of there."

"Well, then, Mr. Sinclair, this explains the note made in her journal entry for Wednesday evening. I found the journal in her purse. The note read, "Perry Sinclair, a real jerk, he's mine. I wish I could have seen him squirm when he heard my message."

"What message would that be?" the commissioner asks.

"I didn't listen to the message until Thursday morning. I had enough of Libby's theatrics on Wednesday evening. I went straight home and turned off my phone. She stated in the message that she is pregnant. I know this doesn't look good. I did not kill Libby," Perry declares firmly.

"I will request the medical examiner to do an autopsy immediately. Meantime, don't leave Canada," demands the commissioner.

"You will have to go to the police department and give them your statement. Please give the assistant commissioner Dr. Fairchild's hotel phone number. This is one call that I am not looking forward to doing."

"I am a district attorney, and I can call Dr. Fairchild."

"That won't be a good idea. You're still a suspect."

Chapter Thirty-One

Perry gives his statement to the assistant commissioner. He signs and dates the statement. He pauses for a moment before standing up to leave. Mixtures of emotions rush through his veins, causing him to feel hollow and disconnected from everyone around him.

He sighs a bit of relief that it isn't Dr. Fairchild who was murdered, but he questions why he doesn't feel more horrible that it is Libby instead. He knows that his next step is to inform Dr. Fairchild of this tragedy.

Chapter Thirty-Two

Dr. Fairchild drops the phone receiver down, shocked and in disbelief over the phone call. The voice of a robotic operator garbles through, insisting, "Please hang up if you wish to make a call."

Dr. Fairchild puts the receiver on the phone to silence the irritating voice.

"Paddy is too young to be dead. Why didn't I go and see him when he asked. I am such a fool," Dr. Fairchild wails these words through a fountain of tears.

Her phone rings. She ignores the call. The answering machine kicks on and it's Perry.

"Bailey, I need to talk to you."

"Perry, it's me," Dr. Fairchild shouts as she grabs the phone receiver. A screeching sound rips through the receiver, blasting their ears.

"I am sorry. I'll turn off the machine."

"What's going on?" Dr. Fairchild asks.

"I've some very bad news. Libby was murdered yesterday. It's a mess and I am sure you will be getting a call from Commissioner LaFleur. There's so much I have to tell you, and I don't know where to start. I'm a suspect."

"Why are you a suspect?"

"Libby left me a message saying she's pregnant."

"Oh," Dr. Fairchild's voice drops to a whisper. "I've got to go. I can't endure this. This is just too much. Just before you called, I ended a phone conversation with Clarkson Wade. He is Paddy's attorney. Mr. Wade called to inform me that Paddy passed away this morning and wanted to know how soon I could be in Alabama. He said he needs to talk to me about funeral arrangements and the living trust that Paddy left for me."

"Bailey, I am so sorry for your loss. I know how much Paddy meant to you. When the commissioner calls, let him know that I can take care of everything here, if this is okay with you. I'll do what I can."

"That's fine. But if you're a suspect, it'll be difficult."

"I am not worried. Once the autopsy is completed then, the commissioner will focus on the right suspect. These are just formalities."

"Perry, how did Libby die?" Dr. Fairchild asks.

"She was murdered in your T-Bird. She was beaten and strangled. Libby was using your car to take Mousey to the vet. I guess Mousey was sick and vomiting, and Libby didn't want anything to happen to her on her watch. There was vomit all over the car seat and it stunk of cat elimination. Libby was found by the car wash attendant. I don't know all the details, just what little Commissioner LaFleur shared with me. He found the paperwork in the car from the vet regarding Mousey. The disturbing part of all of this is that Libby was wearing your clothes."

"Bailey, I really need to talk to you about everything. It's just so much has happened in a short period of time."

"Talk to me then. Enough of your sidestepping bullshit. I don't need your crap."

"Libby had me over for dinner the night before she was murdered. When she answered the door, she was wearing your clothes, candles were lit on the staircase, and the table was set for a king. She made us martinis and proceeded with her obsession to impersonate you.

"To say the least, I wasn't impressed. It was disturbing how much she looked and acted like you. I finished my martini and left. Every five minutes, she kept calling my cell phone. I turned the phone off until the next morning. I listened to the message and there was more drama. She said she's pregnant."

"Shit, Perry, do you know how this looks? No wonder you are the number one suspect. Do you think she was pregnant?" Dr. Fairchild asks.

"Honestly, I don't know. I guess I am hoping this is just one of her theatrics."

"When do you expect to hear from the commissioner?" inquires Dr. Fairchild.

"He said that he was having the ME work through the weekend. Bailey, I hate to change the topic, but there's a couple of questions that need to be answered, or, at least, thought of before the commissioner calls."

"Did Mousey have any allergies?"

"It was in the vet report."

"She is highly allergic to shrimp, but Libby knew that. I am confused. None of these make sense. I don't understand why she was wearing my clothes."

"When are you leaving for Alabama?"

"Tonight. I am hoping I can catch a red-eye flight. Where's Mousey?"

"She wasn't in the car. I am sorry, I don't know."

"Please try and find her. Check back at the condo. There's a set of keys in my office under my printer stand. It's in a plastic bag taped underneath the metal slot. Thank you, I must go."

Dr. Fairchild holds back her tears and proceeds to make her flight arrangements. She drops the phone on the glass table top, breaking the glass into pieces.

"Damn it, no!"

"I am so sorry, Paddy. Please forgive me."

Each word for Dr. Fairchild is becoming high and hysterical with grief. The regret of the many times she was too busy for Paddy is now settling in as a permanent emptiness within her soul. A foreboding presence haunts every breath she takes. This isn't the first time she has experienced this ghastly feeling.

Chapter Thirty-Three

Dr. Kendall is startled from a deep sleep. She reaches over and answers the phone.

"Hello, this is Dr. Kendall."

"Good evening, Dr. Kendall, this is Dr. Fairchild. I apologize that I am calling so late. I will be catching the red-eye this evening to Alabama. My grandfather has passed away.

"Korey is working diligently to get the background on the mayor and his nephew. Please continue to work with Korey on the torso case. Commissioner LaFleur will probably be asking you questions about Libby and me. Mr. Sinclair called me to inform that Libby was murdered yesterday."

"Bailey, you have my deepest condolence. I have met with Korey and he gave me some articles on the mayor. I have contacted the Beverly Hills Medical Center, and I am expecting a report from the head plastic surgeon on breast implant surgeries that were performed within the past five years. Commissioner LeFleur called my office and left a message. I haven't had a chance to return his call."

"It sounds like everything is in order. If you need me, I am a phone call away. Thank you for everything. I know a lot has come down your way more than what is expected of you."

"Have a safe flight. Please call me when you get to Alabama. Check in periodically so we'll know you are okay," Dr. Kendall asks.

Chapter Thirty-Four

Dr. Fairchild finishes packing for her trip to Alabama. Many thoughts and emotions are rushing through her mind and soul. The phone rings, and, this time, she decides to answer Korey's call.

"Hello, Korey, how are you?"

"A little concerned. You haven't returned my calls. I have the report on Mayor Sterlino."

Korey's enthusiasm is well delivered. Korey has spent a half hour going over his report.

"Well, I've said enough. What's going on? Usually, you interrupt me about every other sentence or ask me to fast-forward to the facts," remarks Korey.

"You sound excited," Dr. Fairchild whispers.

"Pardon me, I can barely hear you, Bailey. Are you okay?"

"Paddy passed away this morning, and I am leaving tonight on the red-eye. I'll be taking some time off to regroup. Please continue to work with Dr. Kendall. I talked to her this evening, and I told her that I'll be in Alabama for a while. It sounds as though you have enough evidence for an arrest."

"I think so," Korey replies.

"You must be absolutely sure; be thorough. We don't want to botch and lose this case due to lack of substantial evidence. Make sure it's not circumstantial.

"Korey, have Dr. Kendall's assistant schedule a conference call for the three of us tomorrow at 3:00 p.m."

"This is a lot for you to take, the passing of Paddy and what happened to Libby," Korey states.

"It's okay. This has to be done. We'll discuss all the facts that we have and decide on the best way to present them to the Beverly Hills district attorney. This is a direct hit on an influential family with a lot of power and money. We have no room for error."

"Do you need a ride to the airport?" ask Korey.

"No, I am going to call for a cab. But thank you anyway," states Dr. Fairchild.

Dr. Fairchild boards the plane and finds her seat. Tired and heartbroken, she closes her eyes. All her attempts to fall asleep are interrupted by flashbacks of her past conversations with Paddy. Remorse is setting in. She is highly disappointed in herself for displaying such a dismissing behavior towards Paddy. Those two words, "too busy," replay over and over again in her mind.

She fidgets in her seat from side to side, unable to get comfortable. She gives up after a couple of rounds. Sleeping is definitely not happening; on this trip are her restless thoughts. She finally positions herself in the center. Pleasantly pleased that there isn't a passenger in the seat next to her, she removes her personal journal from her briefcase and props it erect into the vacant seat.

Dr. Fairchild flips to the last entry in her journal and notices that the page has a coffee stain starting in the middle, with drip lines being maneuvered by the crinkles to the bottom of the page. She is astounded over the stain because she is very careful, and she doesn't remember spilling any coffee on the page.

She shrugs this off as another side effect from long hours of work and lack of sleep. She turns the page and just stares into the white sheet. All her feelings and emotions that used to flow so easily won't go beyond the pen; there are no words for the entry. She closes the journal and gently puts it back into the briefcase.

The sadness of losing Paddy is weighing heavily in her heart. Trying to hold back the tears that are rushing through is impossible. She can't control any emotion that she loses to the flood of tears.

Chapter Thirty-Five

"Good morning, Bailey. I am Clarkson Wade, your grandfather's attorney. This isn't the best way to meet someone. I feel as though I already know you. Paddy raved about you, sometimes endlessly. He was quite proud of you. Your grandfather was an interesting old chap. Now, on to the business. This is the envelope he left," states Mr. Wade.

Dr. Fairchild extends her right arm and hand towards Mr. Wade as he approaches her for a handshake. She anticipated something warm and strong from his touch. She assumed this since he was from Texas, but was quite surprised by his effortless gesture of brushing his fingertips briefly over her palm. Mr. Wade stays focused on his mission to deliver Paddy's letter. Now, she sees why Paddy trusted Mr. Wade. It was his deliverance; he is direct and with total focus, just as Paddy was.

"You will notice that the letter is addressed to you marked PERSONAL AND CONFIDENTIAL. He requested that I keep my presence while you open the envelope. I guess, in case you have any legal questions.

"Paddy stressed how important it was for you to receive these documents in case of his death."

Mr. Wade glares into Dr. Fairchild's eyes as he hands her the envelope.

"It is a pleasure to meet you as well."

"Is everything okay? Are you all right? You've practically glared the life right out of me," Dr. Fairchild suspiciously questions.

"Yes, forgive me. I do apologize. I guess I am just curious about the content of the letter.

"What could possibly cause Paddy to act like he just saw a ghost?

"The afternoon before his death, he came into my office frantically. The more I asked him what was wrong, the more nervous he became."

Dr. Fairchild slips the envelope into her black leather handbag.

"I will open the envelope later. Honestly, I don't want to deal with this right now. I promise I will call if I have any questions," states Dr. Fairchild.

"Bailey, are you staying at Paddy's?

"Yes, I need to start making funeral arrangements. And there is a lot of legal matters that I have to get in order. I will probably be here for at least a month or so."

"Let me know if there's anything that I can do?" offers Mr. Wade.

"There is one thing that I would really appreciate. If you would please call the police department and have them bring over to Paddy's the evidence box. I thought I would start trying to figure what exactly happened," Dr. Fairchild requests.

"I thought the coroner declared Paddy's death was accidental due to an overdose of the medication he was on. Is this the forensic expert taking over?

"Maybe this is the time for you to leave your work in Canada," orders Mr. Wade.

"You should know Paddy as well I do. Do you really think Paddy would do anything to cause an accidental death?" Dr. Fairchild asks.

"You know how explicit he is. His mind was too sharp. There's absolutely no way that his death was accidental. I am sure of it."

Dr. Fairchild walks away towards the door.

"Good-bye," she yells. Her voice escalates in volume.

"I'll have the evidence box delivered to Paddy's later this evening," states Mr. Wade, his last words to Dr. Fairchild, an end to an emotional and heated meeting.

Chapter Thirty-Six

Three days earlier...

Paddy bounces around in his old truck as he drives down the driveway to his home and is astonished at the sight of a silhouette image that shadows onto the garage door. He brings the truck to a screeching halt, exits the truck, and walks slowly towards the image. The image fades off the garage door, and a person stands directly in front of Paddy.

"Oh, my God, Snowbird. You look wonderful, beautiful as always. What a relief! At first, all I saw was a silhouette. When did you get in? And why didn't you call and let me know you were coming?

"What a lovely surprise to have you here, Bailey. Would you like some tea?"

"Yes."

She walks away from Paddy and heads towards the house.

Paddy feels something strange about his Bailey. She seems distant. He is always intuitive to her moods, though it's been many years since their last visit.

"You didn't answer my question. When did you arrive?"

"I flew in this morning."

"You have a key. You could have let yourself in!" states Paddy.

The teapot whistle blows while Paddy sets the table for their tea.

"Do you have any brown sugar cubes?" she asks.

"No. When did you start using sugar? That has always been off-limits with you."

She sips her tea and pushes the teacup towards Paddy. She moves away from the table and walks into the living room.

She picks up a blue and white porcelain shoe and examines it as though it was her first time viewing this piece.

"I always loved Grandma's porcelain Victorian shoe collection."

Her recollection gives Paddy chills. Dr. Fairchild never calls her grandmother "Grandma." It has always been "Nannie."

Paddy turns his head, so that she will not see his look of uneasy puzzlement.

Whenever Dr. Fairchild visits Paddy, he always rearrange a piece of Nannie's porcelain shoes and place other clues. And before Dr. Fairchild leaves, she always put the pieces back and let Paddy know what clues she has found. This is a game that they both love to play since Dr. Fairchild was a little girl. The game feeds Paddy's appetite for solving mysteries, a passionate hobby that he loves sharing with Dr. Fairchild.

"Could we please sit in the kitchen?" she asks. "There are some things that I think we should talk about."

"What's wrong? You don't seem yourself."

Paddy stares at her across the table.

"Okay, what's the mystery all about?"

"You really do love Bailey. She's very fortunate to have you in her life and to share such closeness. It's evident with all of her pictures throughout the house."

"What are you talking about? You are Bailey."

"No. I am Rachel Ralston. I was born Rachel Ann Fairchild. You should know you were there when we were born. Your precious daughter, Ann, was giving birth at the age of seventeen. This was a family secret to protect her from the shame of being raped. It must have been heartbreaking when our mother died during childbirth. How angry were you, old man?" Her voice quivers as she tries to control her anger.

"My anger dissipated over the years by the love and joy that Bailey gave me," Paddy states.

"How did you make the decision of which baby to give away?" Rachel's voice crackles with each word.

"That's not what happened. You were stillborn. The doctor and nurse tried everything to get you to breathe. There was no life. The doctor declared your time of death at delivery—stillborn. The nurse took you away."

"What was the reason for no burial?" Rachel asks.

77

"There was. We thought you were buried with your mother. The nurse made the arrangements. The death of your mother and the stillborn baby was too much for your grandmother and me. I thought I was going to lose her as well. We decided not to have your name on the tombstone. I am so sorry."

"What happened to my grandmother?"

"She died when Bailey was three. She never really recovered from the loss of your mother. She lost the will to live. Her health drastically decreased. I raised Bailey. We are very close."

"Why are you staring at me?" Rachel asks.

"It's pretty incredible how identical you both are. I honestly thought you were Bailey," Paddy says.

Paddy walks over to the coat rack and turns the rack ninety degrees, so the emblem with his initials, PF, would face towards the wall.

"What are you doing, old man?" Rachel asks.

"Would you please stop playing with the coat rack? Stop the pacing back and forth. The creeks in the floorboards are gnawing at my nerves like the scratching on a chalkboard. Enough already."

"I am just fiddling around. I guess feeling a little anxious," replies Paddy.

Paddy strolls over towards the fireplace.

"Let's go back to the kitchen. There's more to this story that I want you to know."

He sits at the kitchen table and played with the toothpicks. He is snapping them in half and placing the broken pieces in a row.

"I would rather sit in the living room. These chairs are hard on my back."

"That's fine, let's go."

Paddy props the back of the chair onto the table, balancing on the two front chair legs.

"Have you contacted Bailey? Does she know about you?" Paddy asks.

"No, but she will know in time," Rachel states.

"I will be taking over her life. Because of her I lost my life, everyone who mattered. Five years ago, my husband and son were killed in a plane crash."

"What does that have to do with Bailey?"

"My husband, Dr. Douglas Ralston, was due to be a speaker at her seminar in Canada. He was a forensic anthropologist. We had everything in our marriage, an affluent lifestyle that most would only dream of.

"This has everything to do with Bailey. My family died because of going to see her. Their itinerary was to arrive three days prior to the seminar. Our son was to visit his family in Canada and Douglas was going to meet Bailey before the seminar. They never met.

"After the plane crash, my husband's secretary called me. She needed Bailey's contact information. That's when I discovered that I was an identical twin. I have known for five years.

"Douglas kept all his business information on his computer, including the secret that he stumbled on by accident. In the folder was an e-mail that he sent to Bailey, requesting that he would be a speaker and it was urgent that they meet prior to the seminar.

"Attached to the e-mail was a picture of Bailey. I was probably as shocked as Douglas when he saw the identical twin whom he never knew existed. Douglas did a lot of research. He contacted the nurse that was there during our birth.

"She told Douglas that while she was walking away with me, I faintly gasped, and then the soft little body in the towel moved. She checked my vitals and I wasn't dead. Amazingly, for my sake, she also was paid handsomely by a very wealthy family in Texas to find a baby girl for adoption. This prominent family wanted to keep it quiet. The situation worked out beautifully for the nurse and the Barclay's. My parents were Charles and Elizabeth Barclay. Charles Barclay was an oil tycoon and Mrs. Barclay was a prominent stay-at-home wife.

"The Barclay's were very good to me. They gave me a life that most only dream of, a true fairy tale. I was their only child, and we were very close. They were killed in a plane crash two days after my son was born.

"All I had was my husband and son.

"I followed Bailey's whole life for the last five years, learning all that I could about her career, the infamous Dr. Bailey Fairchild. I even got to know her best friend, her lovers, the police, even her coworkers and her enemies. It's amazing what I've gotten away with by looking identical to her.

"You must be very proud of her?"

"I am."

"I even followed you to Mr. Wade's office. Some legal matters?" questioned Rachel. "You seemed quite nervous."

"I've been receiving some threatening calls and letters."

"I know. That was me," says Rachel.

"Rachel, what do you want from me?"

Rachel walks towards Paddy and puts her hand on his shoulder. She leans into his ear and whispers, "You. Bailey will have to feel the loss of someone whom she loves dearly."

She pulls a revolver from her purse and points at Paddy.

"I know you take nitroglycerin tablets. Let's go upstairs to your bedroom," she demands.

"Can we talk about this?" Paddy asks.

"I am sorry for your loss. You have a family now. There's Bailey and me. There shouldn't have to be revenge." Paddy's fear is imminent in each word.

The sleeping pills that Rachel put in his tea earlier are starting to take effect. Paddy jerks his head while it bobbles up and down, fighting sleep.

"Let's go now," Rachel pushes Paddy towards the stairs, poking the revolver in his back.

"Please get the nitroglycerin. Don't look so surprised, old man, that I know this much about you. It's everything that I must do to be the perfect Bailey.

"The many times that I've been at Bailey's and have had access to all of her belongings, including the keys that she nicely marked as Paddy's, helped with your demise.

"Take these and lie down on the bed."

Paddy is too weak to fight. He turns onto his right side, closes his eyes, and awaits his destiny. He hopes that his trails of clues will help his Snowbird solve his horrible death.

Rachel walks away from Paddy. She turns and glances at him briefly, and then smirks in satisfaction of her newest victim. Her footsteps fade with distance. The front door closes.

Paddy, near unconsciousness and with barely any life left, reaches for the picture of Dr. Fairchild on the nightstand and turns it towards the dresser mirror. A pen lies next to the picture. He proceeds to write on his palm the letters "TW." He clinches his fist tightly and sighs with his last breath of life.

Chapter Thirty-Seven

A new day dawns. Rachel calls 911 from a cell phone.

"Hello, please send the police to Paddy Fairchild's on Dauphin Island."

Click. She disconnects from her call. She tosses Paddy's cell phone out the window.

Chapter Thirty-Eight

There's pressure on Dr. Fairchild's chest. She can barely breathe. The memories of her time with Paddy are overwhelming. The pressure intensifies the farther she drives down Plantation Road. She feels her lungs collapsing, making it impossible to exhale without any pain.

"Forgive me, Paddy. I am so sorry that I never made time for you. I promise I will find out what happened."

She pulls off the road and concedes to her emotions, a hostage to a mixture of tears and anger that held her frozen in time for hours. Dr. Fairchild finally pulls herself together and proceeds to Paddy's on Dauphin Island. Dr. Fairchild enjoys taking the ferry over to Dauphin Island. The fresh air and the waves are very tranquil. She isn't sure of what to expect once she arrives. It has been many years.

Entering into Paddy's house seems intrusive to Dr. Fairchild. Instantly, memories of the past flood through her mind, swarming around uncontrollably.

It is hard for Dr. Fairchild to go through each room with the yellow crime scene tape reminding her of her loss.

She sits in Paddy's favorite leather recliner and embraces memories of her and Paddy when she was a little girl. One of her favorite memories is when they would play finding clues that Paddy would leave throughout the house. For some reason, Dr. Fairchild tries to avoid her hardest task to collect evidence of what transpired before Paddy's death.

Dr. Fairchild startles when her cell phone vibrated off the table from an incoming call.

"Hello," she answers softly.

"Hey, beautiful, it's Korey. I am checking on you. I haven't heard from you in a couple of days. Are you all right? Bailey!" Korey shouts.

"You don't need to shout. I am here. I am not as strong or altogether as everyone thinks that I am or should be," replies Dr. Fairchild.

"What are you talking about?" Korey asks.

"I've never said that or implied it."

Dr. Fairchild's voice grows husky as she continues spilling her feelings.

"And I'm horrible at my job. If I was so wonderful and so great at solving these crimes, giving up so much of my precious time, the dedication and devotion to this so-called career that I love, then damn it, I should have been here for Paddy. It's my fault he is dead."

"You know it's not your fault. I can be there in six hours," states Korey.

"No, I'll be okay. How's the Beverly Hills plastic surgeon?" Dr. Fairchild asks.

"We've run into some road blocks. Their power, money, and connections are keeping us at bay for the moment.

"The heat seems to have cooled off from District Attorney Perry Sinclair. He said Libby's killer is still at large, and he has been cleared.

"While we are on this subject, this is one of the reasons why I'm calling. It seems that your DNA was found at the crime scene."

"Obviously, it's my car and my DNA would be in the car," states Dr. Fairchild.

"Yes, it's obvious for hair and fingerprints. But your blood was on the broken window. You have the perfect motive. Your fiancé was her lover."

"Come on, Korey. You know as well as I do that I am over him. Why not Perry? He has a more convincing motive than I do. She was pregnant with his baby."

"Anyway, it's impossible. I wasn't there. I was in New Jersey," Dr. Fairchild replies defensively. "Where is this going?"

"You're in the midst of a murder investigation as a prime suspect. You've been working with the medical examiners both in Canada and New Jersey in trying to understand the mind of a serial killer who's been at large for the last five years. And now, the death of Paddy. So, I don't know. You tell me where this is all going. I'd like to think that your life is not in danger," Korey says indignantly, all in one breath.

Then he scolds Dr. Fairchild. "Matter of fact, it would be okay for you to admit that you can be vulnerable and possibly even scared. It's okay for Bailey not to portray the perfect human being that she thinks she must be all the time."

"I got it. Thank you for being a wonderful friend and the best colleague. I've changed my mind. If you are not needed by Dr. Kendall, I'll take up your offer to come here.

"Would you please give me a couple of days to grieve alone?" Dr. Fairchild asks. "Thanks for calling. I'll see you soon."

Dr. Fairchild struggles to control her quavering. She hangs up.

Chapter Thirty-Nine

The ferry ride from Dauphin Island to the mainland isn't as pleasant as she has anticipated. The water is rough, slapping the waves hard against the side of the ferry. But it's still tranquil for Rachel. She mediates her thoughts back to the scene at Paddy's. The surprise look on his face was priceless once he realized that she wasn't his precious Bailey.

With a deep breath, she feels the cold, misty dew air that embraces itself upon her face. The ferry rocks back and forth as it embarks the pier.

All passengers are herded like sheep to the only exit off the ferry. A little motion sickness and with sea legs, Rachel wonders aimlessly through the parking lot, looking for her car. The car search was a success. Rachel nestles back into the car seat, turns on the engine, and slowly drives the car out of the stall, amazed at how wonderful she feels. This is a guarantee after each killing.

Just when she starts to accelerate, a man wearing a trench coat appears out of nowhere and taps the hood of the car. Startled, Rachel slams on the brakes, and the car screeches to a stop. He moves his body to the driver's window and bangs aggressively. Apprehensive, Rachel slowly rolls down the window.

"How may I help you?" Rachel fearfully asks.

"Dr. Fairchild, sorry for my abruptness. I would like to talk to you. It's urgent."

"Do I know you?"

"Not really, indirectly you might say."

"Okay, who are you and what's so important that you nearly had me run you over. Not to mention that you scared the crap out of me," Rachel avows.

"I'm Inspector Julian Grenier with the Montreal Police Department. I have some information that I need to go over with you regarding your assistant, Libby Grayson's murder."

"I am sorry. I can barely hear you over the sirens," Rachel states deceitfully, knowing that the police are heading to Dauphin Island.

Rachel intuitively moves the inspector along; it was getting a little too close for comfort at this point. Rachel cogitates.

The inspector repeats the comment that was drowned out by the sirens.

"Would it be possible for us to meet later this evening?" Inspector Grenier asks.

"Yes, what do you have in mind?"

"There's Jake's Place, a restaurant next to the hotel where I am staying. It's off Plantation Road. Would eight o'clock tonight work for you?"

"That would be fine. Which hotel did you say you were staying at?"

"I didn't, but I am at the Marriott. Curiously, why does it matter?"

"It doesn't. I am just curious."

"Until later."

Inspector Grenier walks away.

This encounter with the inspector has agitated Rachel more than she thinks could be possible. She arrives at her hotel and briskly walks to her room. Full of anxiety, she paces back and forth for at least twenty minutes, speculating what information could the inspector have that would prompt him to follow her from Canada to Alabama; more concerned of why he has been following her or, as he thinks, Dr. Fairchild.

It's six thirty, and Rachel isn't thrilled about her dinner date.

"I have to do something. I can't risk anything or take any chances that will uncover that I am not Bailey," mumbles Rachel.

Chapter Forty

There's a knock on the inspector's hotel room door. He looks in the peephole and proceeds to open the door.

"Oh, this is a pleasant surprise. Please come in."

Two gunshots are fired. The inspector holds onto the door while holding his chest. His limp body drops to the floor and lies in a pool of blood. A cigar is still in his mouth; he is dead.

Rachel runs to the stairway, pauses to collect herself, and then proceeds to the garage. Calmly, she walks towards the main street. The two blocks to her car seems an eternity. She unlocks the door and slides in. She looks in the rearview mirror, ruffles her hair, and smiles with satisfaction of her last deed.

Exhausted from her day's events, she goes back to the hotel where she can plan her encounter with Dr. Fairchild. Rachel decides it's best that she stay quiet for a while. She holds the picture of her husband and son close to her heart, embracing them while she cries herself to a slumber. Plans for Dr. Fairchild will have to wait.

Chapter Forty-One

Korey arrives at Paddy's to support Dr. Fairchild during her grieving time. Dr. Fairchild is sitting in a white wicker chair, wrapped in a blanket. The nights are usually cooler in late summer. Korey approaches Dr. Fairchild with a big smile.

"Hey gorgeous, I am glad to see you. Thanks for asking me to be here for you.

"Alabama is different. You will have to elaborate and explain to me why you love this place so much. It's so not you. You are refined, classy, and full of sophistication. I am just a little surprised," affirmed Korey.

"Nice to see you, too. You sound a little snobbish and judgmental."

"I don't mean to. This is so not you," gravels Korey.

"Let's go inside. There's a lot we need to talk about. We need to discuss the New Jersey case that is a priority."

"I know. This has been a horrible time for you. "Are you sure you are ready to tackle business at this time?"

"Most definitely. Believe it or not, it's what I need to get through this period of grieving.

"Thanks for your concern. I will be okay. We have to stop these killings. And I am feeling the pressure.

"I had the local police bring over the evidence. When I was a little girl, Paddy and I would play a game where he would leave clues throughout the house. I'd find them, and then I would have to tell Paddy what the clues meant. We had a lot of fun."

"You were very close."

"Very close. Paddy and my grandmother raised me when my mother died during childbirth. My grandmother died when I was three, and it's been Paddy and I ever since.

"Korey, I honestly don't believe Paddy's death was an accident. I know that in all of these evidences, he left clues. I am sure of it," Dr. Fairchild confidently states.

"Have you found any?"

"I haven't started. That's where you come in. I thought we could do this together. And I promise I will tell you a little about me growing up in Alabama."

"Oh, really, that's one way to get a guy to bite."

"Maybe even share some of my skeletons."

"Bailey has skeletons? Who'd think that? You are too perfect."

"I said 'I might share.' You're being a smart ass. Would you like a tour of the house?"

"Sure."

Dr. Fairchild guides Korey through each room, and then stops at Paddy's bedroom. She glares at the yellow crime ribbon that decorates Paddy's bedroom.

"We don't have to do this now," states Korey.

"I am okay."

Dr. Fairchild walks in the bedroom and scans her surroundings. She stands at the tip of the tape that is on the floor outlining the silhouette of where Paddy's body lay.

"Let's start with the kitchen. This is where we started all our games."

"Before we start, we need to talk about your loss. Paddy was your world and you are diving right into the business mode. This isn't normal or healthy," Korey points out.

"Oh, now you are a shrink," Dr. Fairchild sneers.

"Now, who's the smart ass?" retorts Korey.

"That was unfair and rude of me. I am sorry."

Dr. Fairchild's bottom lip starts to quiver. A teardrop trickles down her cheek. She is trying to deny her feelings from surfacing. Finally, after acknowledging her loss, she weeps. Through the crying, she tries to speak.

"Losing Paddy hurts so much that I can't bear it. I'd rather keep from crying. I must stay strong for me to prove that his death wasn't an accident."

She stops whimpering to wipe her running nose and turns away from Korey.

He holds her from behind and whispers softly into her ear, "I'm here and we will get through this for Paddy."

Korey turns Dr. Fairchild to face him. He kisses a tear that has rested on her cheek.

"I know Paddy would be so proud of you."

"There's more to my sorrow than his death. I was horrible to him. There were so many times he would call and wanted to talk or hoping I would be coming home soon. He was lonely, and he missed me."

"Maybe it seems worse than what it is."

"My reaction was always too busy or I am involved in a case. The worse part of all of this is he begged for me to come home for my birthday. He said he had a surprise for me."

"I really think you are being too hard on yourself. Paddy knew the type of work you did and what it entailed."

"I didn't share all the details of the cases with him. I didn't want Paddy to worry. The 1934 Model T Ford was that surprise. That car was in our family for three generations. So, you see, I feel like a monster.

"When the police officer told me that Paddy's death was accidental due to an overdose, it crossed my mind that it was my fault.

"How much did I break his heart? How do I forgive myself if that is true?"

Dr. Fairchild's emotions and guilt are causing her to feel faint and vulnerable.

"From all the things you've told about Paddy, he knew how hard you worked. And the only way you could be the best in your field was to give the time that you did."

"Thanks, I won't be at ease until I know for sure."

"I agree with you. I don't believe his death was accidental either. So let's prove it and find out who else may have been involved and why. "

"I need to freshen up a bit," Dr. Fairchild comments.

Dr. Fairchild enters the bathroom; it was cold. The warm water splashed on her face felt refreshing. She reached for a towel, but the towel bar was empty.

"Korey, there is something odd in here."

"What's that?"

"This is unusual. Paddy always had a hand towel on each of the towel bars with our monograms 'PF' and 'BF' side by side. The 'BF' isn't here.

"He always wanted to be sure my towel was out, in case I came for a visit. He would have never taken it off. I think we have found one of Paddy's clues."

"Maybe it was dirty and he washed it."

"I am telling you that may be the case for other people, but not for him. He was methodical. This is going to be a late night. Where are you staying?"

"I haven't made any reservations. I was waiting to get your recommendations."

"There's plenty of room here. In the back is a guest cottage fully equipped with all the necessities, or there's an extra bedroom in the house."

"Will you be able to stay here?" Korey asks.

"Yes, this way I will be able to get familiar with the surroundings. Hopefully, get a sense of what happened. I believe Paddy would want me here."

"I will stay in the guest bedroom, in case you need me."

"I still have funeral arrangements to make. He only wants a simple service and a closed casket. His belief was party when you are alive and no fussing when you're gone."

"If I can be of any help, let me know what to do."

"The service will be this Friday."

Chapter Forty-Two

Alarmed out of a deep sleep by a loud ring, Korey answers the phone, eyes bleary.

"Hello."

"Good morning. I am Mr. Wade, Paddy's attorney. Is Bailey available?"

"One moment please, I will check for you." Korey rolls off the couch and walks to the kitchen where Dr. Fairchild is pouring herself a cup of coffee. Korey is staying with Dr. Fairchild at Paddy's home.

"Bailey, the phone is for you, it's Mr. Wade."

"Good morning, what can I do for you?" Dr. Fairchild asks.

"I am calling to see if there is anything you need, or, if you opened the envelope, whether there were any questions regarding the contents."

"Well, I don't have any questions because I haven't opened the envelope. If you have a minute, I can get the envelope and read it now while you are on the phone."

"That would be fine. I'll hold."

Dr. Fairchild searches her purse. There's no envelope. She looked on the dresser and still no envelope.

"Mr. Wade, I apologize. I am unable to find the envelope. I must have misplaced it. I will look some more, and, when I find it, I will call you."

"I saw you put it in your purse."

"That is true, and I don't remember removing the envelope from my purse. But there has been so much going on, no telling what could have happened to it.

"I better go. I will see you at the funeral. It is on Friday."

"I'll see you then. Good-bye," says Mr. Wade.

Dr. Fairchild continues to search the house and the car. There's still no letter. Confused that she doesn't remember removing anything from her purse, she dismisses this for now. The smell of scrambled eggs with onions, bacon, and fresh coffee has distracted Dr. Fairchild from the search for the envelope. Her taste buds are aroused by the aroma.

"Are you hungry?"

"Mmmm mmmm, yes, I am. Korey, breakfast is fantastic. Thank you."

"There were some interesting things that I noticed in the kitchen."

"Like what?" Dr. Fairchild inquires.

"For instance, did Paddy always put one chair leaned up against the table balancing on two legs?

"There were toothpicks on the table, lined in a row, and a teacup with your name on the front."

"Where was the teacup?"

"On the stove."

"Also, why didn't the police take the teacup as evidence?"

"Good question. Why didn't they? Do you think these are clues from Paddy?"

"I would think so. Let's go into the front room. Paddy was very meticulous. He kept everything in place."

Dr. Fairchild sits in the overstuffed leather recliner and surveys the room. The coat rack caught her eye.

"That's odd. The coat rack is turned around. Paddy's jackets are against the wall, not facing outward. It doesn't make any sense to hang coats behind the rack. Also, his initials on top of the rack are reversed. Instead of 'PF' they are 'FP.'"

"Now that you have pointed it out, it's strange. Bailey, could the reversed letters 'FP' mean fireplace?"

"That's a possibility. I don't see anything that's out of the ordinary."

"There's only a picture of you on the mantle facing the mirror. I'd say a little peculiar. Did you go through any of the evidence from the crime scene?"

"No, I have been avoiding spending anytime in Paddy's room and reading the report."

Dr. Fairchild studies the tape outlining where Paddy's body was on the bed.

"Korey, this report is contradictory. It states that there's tape on the floor indicating where his body was found. But then, two paragraphs later, it's written that he was found facing the dresser on the left side of the bed."

"What in the hell!" Korey exclaims.

"Look at this. Your picture on the dresser is again facing the mirror. There has to be a message here from Paddy. You just don't have pictures showing the backside."

"Something else doesn't make sense with the report. See this spot on the floor next to the outline? It's not mentioned in the report. It stinks like vomit."

"Are you sure?"

"Definitely. I've just read it three times. This investigation was sloppy, a botched job, and rushed for whatever reason. The report states that there were initials 'TW' on Paddy's left palm."

"Do you know of anyone with the initials TW?"

"No, and I don't recall Paddy ever mentioning anyone either."

"There was no mention of a pen in the report. If he wrote with something, it has to be here."

"I see something under the nightstand. It's a pen."

"Bag it and we will do our own evidence testing. We'll keep this quiet. Well, it's nice to see that the local police haven't changed in twenty years. Botched jobs are their specialty," Dr. Fairchild states sarcastically.

"You sound as though you've had some previous experience with the Alabama police. Did you work with them on a case before?"

"No. But we'll continue this conversation later."

"I want to stay focus on Paddy's clues. He's trying to tell us something. Korey, please set up an evidence board downstairs. Make two columns. In one column, write all the evidence, and, parallel to the other column, write a "C" for circumstantial or "H" for hard evidence. And we may need a second board for Dr. Huntington, same concept as well."

"We have to act soon on the Huntington case. I can work with Dr. Kendall. We can't let this slimeball get away with such a gruesome murder. We are so close on this one. I know Paddy's death was unexpected."

"I agree with you. Work with Dr. Kendall to finish up the Huntington case. Plan to leave after the funeral services.

"On the column for the evidence, list the clues as well. And maybe we can find the motive to murder Paddy."

"Is this where we are going, murder?"

"Yes, murder," Dr. Fairchild declares.

"In column one, list the clues and what they mean. The six toothpicks are six clues: Bailey's teacup is a female; the leaning chair is danger; no BF initial monogram towel signifies a female; Paddy's initials reversed on the coat rack indicates the fireplace; Bailey's picture on the mantle facing the mirror, not sure; Bailey's picture with her grandmother on the nightstand facing the mirror on the dresser could indicate the killer knew her; the letters 'TW' written on the palm of his hand is still a question; and the spot on the floor that is not mentioned in the police report. The only fingerprints were Paddy's throughout the house.

"I know. You're probably thinking that these clues don't make any sense, that they are stupid and a little eccentric. But when does any murder case make any sense?"

"Yes, I agree, it doesn't make any sense. The clues are stretching a bit. There are no facts. And only you know what the hell Paddy is trying to say. The only part of this investigation that is factual is we don't have any hard evidence."

"That's exactly why the pictures of me are turned the way they are. As ironic as it may seem, it is why I believe he was murdered. I just don't know by whom," Dr. Fairchild cries out of frustration. Dr. Fairchild recollects her emotions.

"Korey, if Paddy was in a situation where he couldn't be alone or able to write down anything, the only way he could communicate would be to leave his clues."

"I guess it makes sense. And what if for some reason you weren't involved in the case, what would have happened?"

"That's a horrible thought to bear, knowing his killer got away with it."

"Would you please bag pieces of the stain on the floor as evidence for testing?"

"I already did. Changing the subject?" Korey replies.

Dr. Fairchild smiles with delight. Korey's efficiency pleases her.

"That was a pretty sight. I haven't seen that in a while."

"What's that?"

"Your smile," says Korey.

"I am not going to apologize for Paddy's clues again. This is what we have to work with, and it would be best if you would put your energy into the case."

"Wow, you need to step off this roller coaster. I have never seen you so out of touch with reality."

"What are you insinuating?"

"Damn it, Bailey, you are too close. You are brilliant in your field. Losing Paddy is eating you up. I have no problem working on this case even with the weird clues."

"We need to add a third column: the motive."

"You are so damn stubborn. Fine, I tried," Korey states angrily.

There's a knock at the door. Korey answers the door with vigilance.

"I'm Detective Rowlands with the Alabama Police Department."

Dr. Fairchild hears the conversation and walks to the door.

"Please come in. How may I help you?"

"Well, a body was found yesterday at a hotel. He was shot."

"What does this have to do with me?"

"Nothing really. Only that he was an inspector from Montreal. Do you know Inspector Grenier?"

Detective Rowlands continues his interrogation.

"I know you are here for Paddy's death. I am sorry for your loss. I would visit with him occasionally at his bait shop. He would always talk about his granddaughter, the forensic anthropologist who lives in Canada. I just assumed there would be a connection."

"Is his killer at large?" Korey asks.

"This is my colleague, Korey Scott. He works with me on cases. We are working on the investigation report on Paddy's murder."

"Yes, the killer is at large," responds the detective.

"I thought Paddy's death was declared accidental. I didn't mean to interrupt what you were working on. Did you say you know Inspector Grenier?"

"I never said that I did, and I don't know him," Dr. Fairchild answers.

"Before I go, Paddy still has your paintings hanging in the bait shop. Some talent you have there. Do you still paint? You went to some fancy art school in France."

Dr. Fairchild avoids any further conversation on her painting.

"Sorry, Detective, but we need to continue on with our investigation."

"Here's my card. If you remember anything about the inspector, please call me."

"There's nothing to remember. As I said earlier, I don't know him."

The detective leaves, and, as he walks away from the house, he turns back and stares at Dr. Fairchild for a moment. He spits a wad of gum onto the walkway. Dr. Fairchild observes his repellent behavior.

"God, he is an obnoxious slug," Dr. Fairchild affirms.

"Korey, do you have any idea why an inspector from Canada would he here?"

"Only if he was working on Libby's murder."

"Tomorrow, would you please call the Montreal Police and see what you can get from them? It still doesn't make any sense why he would be here. All he had to do was call me, if I were the reason for him to be in Alabama."

"And there's more of the mystery puzzle of Bailey. So, I didn't know you painted, let alone studied in France. I guess I will never know everything about you. You are intriguing and full of surprises. When are you going to tell, or were you?"

"While I am here, I would like to go to the bait shop and see your paintings. It's odd thought that Paddy hung them in a bait store."

"It's not like that. Paddy bought a small shop next door and made it into a gallery. He loved fine art. He had other famous artists, not just mine.

"Paddy tried to bring refinement and some sophistication to Dauphin Island. It's different than the mainland. He wanted to introduce the beauty of art to the island. Believe it or not, he did sell some nice pieces. He loved my paintings. I don't think he would sell them."

"I am curious. Why did you stop painting?"

"That's another long story that I promise we will discuss someday; it correlates with the Alabama police."

"Great. Thanks for really getting my curiosity aroused."

"There's a part of me that I do keep hidden for a reason. In time, I will explain," Dr. Fairchild promises.

"We should get back to the evidence board. After the visit from the detective, the only person of interest is me. I am the connection to Paddy and to the inspector from Canada. I just don't know why they are connected. This is what we have to figure out."

"The inspector, was he working on Libby's murder?"

"It's ludicrous. I wasn't even in Canada when she was murdered."

"Your DNA was in the car."

"Korey, that is possible since the car is mine. It's an obvious setup, but by whom?" Dr. Fairchild wonders.

"I agree."

"Please call Dr. Kendall tomorrow and have her send to me Libby's investigation and autopsy reports.

"I think we will need to expand the evidence boards. These three cases are all connected. I feel there is a serial killer. Now, we have to find this person before there are more deaths.

"Would you like to take a break and see the gallery slash bait shop?"

"That would be nice."

"It's actually not far from here. We can walk. There's a great seafood restaurant, The Harbor Cove. We can have dinner afterwards."

Korey approaches Dr. Fairchild. He leans towards her to give her a hug. Dr. Fairchild starts to relax in his arms and then pulls back.

"Korey, I am not ready."

Lori Howell

"Not ready for what? I am not approaching you for a wild interlude. Just giving a friend a hug whom I thought needed one. Sorry, it won't happen again."

Chapter Forty-Three

Part of what Korey says is true; the other part, he would have made love to Dr. Fairchild. He has always been attracted to her.

"The restaurant is just a few blocks past the ferry terminal," Dr. Fairchild says.

The seaweed scent, entwined within the salty dew, nestles on her cheeks, rejuvenating all of her senses. The fresh air energizes her tired body and mind.

This is what I needed; a walk and the fresh air.

She feels bad that she rejected Korey's hug. Her vulnerability holds her hostage from feeling.

Since her heartbreak from Perry, she's reluctant to give her heart to another man. The thought of opening up and trusting someone new turns her cold inside.

"Well, what do you think of Paddy's idea of a gallery and a bait shop side by side?"

"It's different, but intriguing."

Korey enters the gallery and is amazed. The outside doesn't reflect the interior.

"This is incredible. Show me your paintings."

"Over here."

Korey follows Dr. Fairchild through an atrium adjacent to the bait shop.

"Impressive. Paddy has created two different worlds. I am still in awe over the bait shop slash art gallery. Did he do well?"

"As you can see, most of the paintings left are the ones that I created. The bait shop has always done very well."

"Why do you think the community didn't buy your paintings?"

"It's not that they didn't offer to buy, Paddy couldn't part with them. There were paintings from all over the world in the gallery.

Paddy's goal was to bring sophistication to Dauphin Island. I believe he did accomplish his mission."

"In honor of his memory, I am thinking about opening a gallery with his paintings."

"Bailey, you painted this Mona Lisa?"

"I tried. It was my art class protégé. We had to pick a famous painting and try to recreate."

"You did an astonishing job. I am amazed how you captured such a likeness. Your Mona Lisa looks like the real thing."

"Thank you."

"Why did you even stop? You have a wonderful talent."

Korey continues his journey into the fine art.

I am in awe over her hidden talent. She is full of surprises. I didn't think it would be possible for me to fall deeper in love with her. The more I am around her, the harder it is for me to suppress my feelings. I don't know if I am able to endure another rejection. These bewildering thoughts dazzle in Korey's mind.

"Hey, over there, you are really engrossed in another world," says Dr. Fairchild.

"I'm really impressed with your paintings. You captured everything; the details are enchanting. This is the Grand Canal in Venice. It's remarkable how well you captured the buildings embedded within the backward 'S' curve. I stayed at the Carlton located in the center of the curve," says Korey.

"My favorite painting is the Mona Lisa. They are all beautiful. The girl stole my heart with that legendary smile."

"Funny. Are you ready to check out the bait shop?" Dr. Fairchild asks.

"This is different. It's organized and all the items that are needed for fishing are here. Paddy doesn't skimp on anything. I guess I am not much for fishing. I'd rather eat them. And speaking of eating, I am hungry. Shall we go?"

"Sure."

Dr. Fairchild walks up to Korey and flashes the most brilliant white smile accented by the deepest dimples.

"Thanks for being here and being a great friend."

The aroma from the bright pink lobster savored by butter and garlic lingers, suppressing drool that caused an ache behind their ears.

"Dinner was wonderful," says Korey.

"I guess you were hungry. You were quiet."

"When we get back, we will need to start working on the evidence board."

"Would you be able to start without me? I would like to review the report that Dr. Kendall sent. I have to focus and get my mind back to work."

"That's fine."

"But before we go in the house, let's go into the garage. I haven't been in there since I have been back."

"Is there anything in particular that you are looking for?"

"No. Just old memories to help me move forward."

They entered the garage. The garage is as organized as the bait shop and gallery. There is a section for tools on one wall, gardening on the other, and Dr. Fairchild's painting materials neatly arranged covered by a tarp.

"What's behind this?" Korey asks as he lifts up the tarp. Under the tarp was a painting of a woman looking into a pond, only an outline in black and white.

"Who's this?"

"My grandmother, and the reflection is a little girl, me. I didn't get a chance to add color."

"If my opinion matters, it's beautiful just the way it is. You brought her beauty out, her dimples and high cheek bones. You can see the passion in your art. I see where you got your stunning smile."

"I never thought of it that way. Good eye."

"Do you miss painting?"

"I used to…a lot. A career in forensics doesn't give you much time for any passionate hobbies. It was my love when I lived here. After I left, everything changed in my life, mostly me."

"I sense there's a mystery or a secret that is hidden deep inside you. Will you ever share this with me?"

"Honestly, I don't know. Maybe in time. Something did happen many years ago and it changed the course of my life."

Korey snoops further into the garage and pulls back another tarp.

"Wow, look at this beauty. Is this the 1938 Model T Ford that you were talking about?"

"Actually, it's a 1934. And, yes, it was my great grandfather's."

"It looks like it is in mint condition."

"That was Paddy. He knew how much it meant to his dad and said one day that it would be mine. I'd rather it have been for different circumstances. Growing up, Paddy made a tradition. Every Sunday, we went for a ride across Dauphin Island. As soon as we got home, he washes the ocean residue from the body of the car."

"It seems as though you have a treasure of memories right here."

Korey slithered graciously onto the leather seat. He gently strokes the wooden dashboard and glides his fingers beneath a metal box. He opens the metal box. Inside is a card addressed to Dr. Fairchild.

"This is for you."

Dr. Fairchild opens the envelope. It's a birthday card from Paddy.

My dearest Bailey,

A little something for my "Snowbird." I know how much this car meant to you. I had so much fun sharing and creating memories—the years watching you grow from my little girl to a woman that I am so proud of. Thank you for all the joy and wonder you gave me. Check out the license plate: "SNOWBRD."

My love forever,
Paddy

Dr. Fairchild tries to hold back her tears. Her throat throbs with pain from choking on words that she can't express. She reads the license plate, and tears flood her cheeks. The pain and her weakness, she lets loose. She falls onto the hood of the car and wails.

"Korey, he is really gone. I can't imagine my life without Paddy. I was so awful to him before my birthday. He called, and, as always, I didn't have time for him."

She cries uncontrollably. Korey gently pulls her towards him, kisses her tears away and holds her in his arms. They snuggled in the front seat. He held her for over an hour. Her running nose and tears soiled his shirt. Korey never flinched. He felt Dr. Fairchild's sobbing vibration across his chest.

"How long have I been a blubbering idiot?"

"Over an hour. You are not a blubbering idiot.

"The car is gorgeous. He calls you 'Snowbird.' Paddy was a remarkable man. He really loved you. I have learned so much about you in just one day, more than the five years we have worked together."

"Today has been an overwhelming day. There are definitely a lot of wonderful memories.

"Look in the ignition. Paddy left the keys. He thought of everything."

"Let's go to the house and start working. Tomorrow afternoon, we will take a ride in the Model T. We both need some fun."

"Handsome, thanks again."

Chapter Forty-Four

"Bailey, there is something puzzling about these cases. They have taken place in three different locations: Canada, New Jersey, and Alabama. Look at the time frames. Libby is murdered in Canada at the time you were in New Jersey. While you were in New Jersey, Paddy dies. Your DNA is at the crime scene in Canada."

"What are you saying?"

"It appears to be a serial killer. Libby was strangled; New Jersey case, she was decapitated; and Paddy was an accidental overdose."

"Don't forget number four. There are four. The inspector, he was shot."

"Bailey, the evidence points to a serial killer."

"What's the motive?"

"I believe these killings are not at random. There's no motive. You're the target. It's revenge."

"Revenge."

"Can you think of anyone?"

"I have solved many cases and have made enemies in the process. I wouldn't know where to start.

"If your theory is true, the only common dominator is Libby and Paddy. They both were in my life. New Jersey was a case that I was asked to investigate."

"You were attacked and evidence disappeared in the middle of the investigation."

"It doesn't make sense," states Dr. Fairchild.

"It does if you are the only target."

"Me, I don't understand why this case or any other would be so personal."

"We have to go back into old cases and see who could be angry enough to want to harm you."

"If it's me they are after, why kill Libby and Paddy? They have done no harm to anyone."

"The evidence points to you as a suspect, a frame-up. This is a cat and mouse game to them. And when the game stops being fun or entertaining, it will escalate.

"Each murder is getting shorter and shorter between each killing. Time is of the essence. I don't want anything to happen to you."

"Nor you or anyone else. Others could be in danger."

"Bailey, please take this seriously. You are in danger."

"I am more certain now that Paddy's death was not accidental; he was murdered. We have to figure out his clues. He knew the killer," Dr. Fairchild declares.

"Don't forget that the inspector knew as well. He was here from Canada pursuing his hunches."

"We need to know why he was here."

"I have his report here. The officer described him wearing a trench coat and stated that he had a cigar in his mouth when he died."

"Is he the man who followed you to New Jersey? You said you smelt stale cigar like the one at your condo when you were attacked last year.

"If this is him, we need to know why he has been trailing you. He is a critical piece in this puzzle. The inspector knew something obviously important enough that got him killed."

"The inspector is a common denominator. He was at all three crime scenes. He may have been at the shooting in the lab with Dr. Kendall. We found cigar butts in the corridor. The same cigar butts in the mayor's office in New Jersey."

"Tomorrow, I will review Paddy's clues. Please contact the Montreal police. See if they can tell you anything about the inspector; what cases he was working on. Call Perry. Have him use his district attorney influence. We need to pull all resources."

"We will find this psycho before we are left with another corpse," reassures Korey.

Chapter Forty-Five

"I called Perry and left him a message."

"That's great. Are you ready to go over the clues? Let's start in the kitchen."

"What did the teacup represent?" Korey asks.

"Female."

"What would indicate a male?"

"A mug. Sturdy and heavier."

"Interesting, I can see how you had fun playing this as a kid.

"The coat rack leads us to the fireplace. Your picture is facing the mirror on the mantle. So far, our mystery person is a woman.

"Don't forget the chair leaning up against the table. What did this mean?"

"Danger!"

"Your picture is facing the mirror on the dresser. The letters 'TW' were written on his palm. Do you know anyone with the letters 'TW'?"

"No, I can't think of anyone. It's been mind-boggling since I read the medical examiner's report.

"Paddy wouldn't have been careless enough to overdose on nitroglycerin. He would have tried to call 911. The only way he wouldn't have made that call is if the killer waited until Paddy died before leaving the scene."

"Bailey, the phone is for you. It's your cell. It vibrated across the table. Sorry to have answered. It's a Mr. Wade. He wants to speak with you."

"It's okay. Thank you. Mr. Wade, good afternoon. How are you?"

"I am fine. Did you ever get a chance to read what was in the envelope?"

"I hate to admit this. I have misplaced it. I will look for it later. I don't mean to be rude, but I must go. Is there anything else?"

"No. The funeral was nice and simple. Please let me know if there is anything that you need."

"I will. Thank you."

The house phone rings louder than normal, agitating Dr. Fairchild, reminding her how silent the house has become without Paddy.

"Hello," Dr. Fairchild's voice crackles. She swallows to clear her throat.

"How's my girl?"

"Hi, Perry, I'm okay."

"Sorry, I couldn't make the funeral. Is this a bad time to go over what I have uncovered on Libby's case?"

"No."

"I am responding to Korey's message that he left yesterday."

"It's not bad timing. Please go on."

"Libby was wearing your clothes at the time of her death. She was driving your car. The police believe her death was a mistaken identity. They believe the killer was after you."

"Oh, this is troubling, but I am not surprised."

"Remember the conversation we had a couple of weeks ago? I said there were some things that I needed to tell you about Libby. Well, what caused me to flee from my last encounter with Libby was at your condo."

"At my condo?"

"Please let me finish. I know, sleazy. She was wearing your clothes. The dinner and music was exactly how you entertained our dates. Libby made a comment that she felt that if she were you, I would find her irresistible."

"God, Perry."

"There's more. I left. It was too much for me. She left numerous messages saying she is pregnant with my baby."

"What does this have to do with me?"

"You were in the midst of solving the Atlantic City case. Dr. Huntington Jr.—his uncle is a corrupted mayor owned by the mob."

"Perry, I am losing my patience," states Dr. Fairchild.

"I went over your notes when you were attacked in your condo. You stated that there was a man standing at your feet wearing a trench coat, smoking a cigar."

"What did you just say about what he was wearing?" Dr. Fairchild asks.

"A trench coat. You described him as Columbo."

"Perry, the police in Alabama found an inspector who was shot in his hotel room. He was wearing a trench coat and died with a cigar in his mouth."

"What was he doing in Alabama?"

"My only guess is me. I don't know why. I haven't figured out how Libby's death and Paddy's are connected."

"It must be connected to the case in Atlantic City. You said the mayor is owned by the mob, and he was protecting his nephew."

"Killing Libby and Paddy is a warning. I don't like this. You are in danger."

"I've been hearing that a lot lately."

"Please don't be so flippant," states Perry.

"They have had plenty of opportunities to kill me."

"That's not the game they are playing. The killer is twisted. They like tormenting. It's a sick form of pleasure."

"Well, the one thing that I know—our killer is a woman," says Dr. Fairchild.

"How do you know that?"

"Because of the clues."

"You mean evidence, forensic evidence?"

"No. I mean clues. Paddy left clues, and he left a teacup on the stove."

"You're kidding me. That's your conclusion that it's a woman."

"Yes, please don't sound as though I am crazy," Dr. Fairchild pleads.

"It doesn't make sense. If the mayor has sent someone to take you out, it wouldn't be a woman."

"There are women assassins. Obviously, the least likely to be a suspect.

"There are more clues. We won't go there."

"This is what I have for Korey. The inspector who was murdered was your Columbo. The Montreal police said he was following you since your attack. He didn't understand why you never filed a police report. The inspector always felt you were a person of interest."

"Why was he in my condo? I never called the police. He was the last person I saw before I went out cold."

"That will remain a mystery. No one knows. The police couldn't answer either. What are your plans?"

"Korey will stay here and work with Dr. Kendall on Paddy's case. I am going to Atlantic City to close the Huntington case. I need to have a one-on-one conversation with the mayor. It's time we nail his nephew."

"Let the local authorities handle him. It's too dangerous."

"I'll be fine. He will be more willing to put his nephew away after I present some incriminating evidence against him."

"When are you leaving?"

"Tomorrow morning."

"Promise you will call me as soon as you arrive. Call me every hour, so I'll know you are safe. Would you like me to meet you there?"

"No. Thanks for offering. I will call you. I'll be fine. Talk to you soon, bye."

"Korey, I am leaving for Atlantic City tomorrow."

"New evidence?"

"No, just taking care of something that I should have done before. Will you be okay to continue Paddy's case with Dr. Kendall?"

"That will be fine."

"See if Dr. Kendall can come here."

"I will call Dr. Kendall to see how soon she can be here."

"Thanks. I will call you when I arrive in Atlantic City."

Chapter Forty-Six

Dr. Fairchild arrives in Atlantic City. She hails a cab to the mayor's office. With a mission to be accomplished, she approaches the receptionist with an attitude.

"Is Mayor Sterlino in?"

"Do you have an appointment?"

"No!"

Dr. Fairchild walks by the receptionist and opens the Mayor's office door.

"Excuse me, how may I help you? Who are you?"

"Skip the formalities. You know who I am. Dr. Bailey Fairchild, the one who is going to put your nephew in the gas chamber for murder."

"Doris, call the police," the mayor yells.

"I agree. Please do call the police, so I may inform them of how you have paid a hit man to kill the dock union director smuggling drugs on the freight cars, muscling local merchants for 80 percent of their revenues."

"Okay, never mind. Don't call the police."

"What do you want from me?"

"Your nephew, Dr. Huntington Jr. I know for a fact that you have been covering for him to keep the social image intact for your sister, his mother. He is a cold-blooded killer and I want him.

"If you will come with me to the district attorney's office and give a statement, I will keep you out of jail."

"Is there any way we can keep this quiet, so my sister won't know that it was me who ratted on her son?"

"I am sure that could be arranged."

Two days after Mayor Sterlino's statement, his nephew was arrested for the gruesome murder of his girlfriend.

"Great job. The arrest hit the news. It's big. A guy from a prominent family, a Beverly Hills pretty boy, was arrested for murder," states Korey.

"How did you get the mayor to cooperate?" Dr. Kendall asks.

"I promised he wouldn't spend any jail time. He's out, and he is a monster himself. I kept my word. He spent no jail time. But I didn't promise him safety from the mob.

"I made a couple of anonymous calls and gave the mob some information that directed them to the mayor.

"This case is solved. The nephew is in prison on death row."

"What happened to the mayor?" Korey asks.

"I would say, give them a few days and I bet the mayor will disappear. Justice will prevail."

It's been awhile since Dr. Fairchild has felt some deep satisfaction. She feels her old self resurfacing. Seeing justice prevailing was a real accomplishment. The pain still burns inside of her every time she thinks of Paddy. *Will the pain and emptiness ever go away?*

She calls Korey on his cell phone while snuggling in the oversized goose down comforter.

"Hi, Korey."

"Nice to hear from you. How are you?"

"Okay. I will be flying home tomorrow. See you then. Good night, I am going to bed."

Dr. Fairchild is feeling ecstatic over the capture of the Beverly Hills plastic surgeon. She smiles from ear to ear, imagining what Mayor Sterlino must be going through, how he's trying to bullshit his way out of the rumors. He was part of an evil and gruesome killing that makes her angry whenever she thinks of the young girl whose body was decapitated and pregnant.

Tired and exhausted, Dr. Fairchild's sleep wasn't as sound as she had hoped. She spent most of the night tossing and turning; a little frightened being alone.

Chapter Forty-Seven

"Excuse me," Dr. Fairchild says as she crosses over a passenger to take her window seat. She rest her head onto the back of the seat and closes her eyes. She tries to relax, eliminating all thoughts, allowing her to enter into a state of tranquility. For a moment or two, she felt wonderful to have no emotions or any thoughts. But that came to a sudden end.

"Please make sure your seat belts are tightly fastened. We are ready for takeoff," says the cheerful flight attendant.

Dr. Fairchild knows the routine, but still is startled out of her tranquil moment. She stares out the window and closes her eyes. The man sitting next to Dr. Fairchild nudges her gently.

"Miss, miss we've landed," he says.

I was more tired than I thought. I slept through the entire flight. This was the first for Dr. Fairchild.

As she was departing from the plane, a gentleman hands her a long stem black rose.

"Thank you," she says. *How odd that he would give me a black rose.*

"This isn't from me. I would give a beautiful lady like you a red rose. While you were sleeping, a woman laid the rose on your lap," he says.

"Did you see what she looked like? Do you see her now?"

"No. I don't see her, and I didn't see her face. She was wearing a big round floppy white hat."

"A picture hat?" says Dr. Fairchild.

"Whatever you women call it, round or picture, it was big and floppy," he says. "My wife has a couple. She walked up to the front of the plane," he replies annoyed.

Dr. Fairchild walks back to the plane, but the doors are closed. The crew is gone. This encounter bothers her.

She hails a cab. Her trip back to Paddy's was troubling, anything but relaxing.

"Hey, beautiful, great job on closing the Beverly Hills murder," says Korey.

He greets Dr. Fairchild with a powerful hug and a gentle kiss on her forehead.

"I've missed you. Glad you are back. Why the sourpuss look? I would think you would be jumping up and down with joy. This was a long and dangerous case that you were able to end with justice. The best part was to have the mayor removed from his position."

Dr. Fairchild hands Korey the black rose.

"This was placed on my lap while I was asleep on the plane."

"Does anyone know who left it?"

"A woman."

"Can anyone identify her?"

"No. No one saw her face. She was wearing a big floppy hat."

"A mystery woman, it's some message she sent you."

"Yeah, I know. The black rose means death," she says, her voice quivering with the response.

"Good news. I have made some headway with the clues Paddy left. It is confirmed that his assailant is a woman."

"I wonder if it is the same woman from the plane." Dr. Fairchild asks, "Why are you so sure, Korey?"

"Unless you are missing an earring, I would guess she dropped an earring the day she…" Korey pauses.

"I dare say, go ahead, say it. The day she killed Paddy."

Korey hands a baggie with an earring inside. "Is this yours?"

"Ironic, it is mine. They were my grandmother's. I lost one earring when I was in Atlantic City last year."

"The start of the Beverly Hills murder case," says Korey.

"Yes, it looks that way."

"Look at me, flash that beautiful smile. I know this is a horrible time for you. I am not going anywhere. We will beat this."

"Promise?"

"I promise."

"I can't think of any woman who has a grudge or a vendetta towards me to the point of murder. Was there anything else?"

"No. I am still trying to piece the rest of Paddy's clues. I think we are close," responds Korey.

"I need to call Perry. I promised I would call as soon as I arrived in Alabama. Then we can go over the details."

Dr. Fairchild leaves a message for Perry, relieved that he didn't answer. She doesn't feel like talking about the case or what happened on the plane.

"Here's a cup of coffee mocha."

"Mmmm, I can smell the hazelnut creamer. Thank you."

"You are the only person whom I know likes to add a splash of hazelnut creamer in a coffee mocha."

Korey hands the cup to Dr. Fairchild. Her hand trembles while reaching for the cup.

"Are you okay? You are trembling."

"I guess reality is setting in. Someone wants me dead, and I am scared."

Korey grabs her cup and puts it on the coffee table. He looks intently into her eyes. His big fingers gently stroke her delicate soft lips, slowly caressing her throat, and then slithering down to her breast. Paralyzed by his hypnotic touch, Dr. Fairchild lies motionless, awaiting his next pose of pleasure. He delicately kisses her lips, licking softly and slowly, enticing her erotic side. Korey pulls her close and tight, his heart pounding with passion. The feel of her breast rubbing against his chest causes an erection. He grabs her thigh. Dr. Fairchild grabs his crotch and caresses his package. Trembling is overcome by ecstasy. Their kisses are wild. His tongue dives deep into her mouth. Crazed with lust, they grab and tear each other's clothes off, wildly tossing garments across the room.

Korey kisses her breast and slowly places Dr. Fairchild on the lush velvet sofa. Their naked bodies form one silhouette. He suckles her nipples.

"Make love to me," she whispers in his ear.

She sucks his fingers one by one. He enters her canal, pumping in rhythm with each suckle, thrashing vigorously.

"Harder, Korey, harder."

Korey holds Dr. Fairchild close and tight. She limps into his arms.

"I love you," Korey tells Dr. Fairchild.

Dr. Fairchild kisses his forehead. She gets up and gathers her clothes that scattered on the floor. No words ever come from Dr. Fairchild as she walks away. Korey lies motionless; surprised at Dr. Fairchild's nonresponse.

Will she ever love me? Why do I continue this charade? Was this one-sided? Did I take advantage of Bailey being vulnerable and scared? This should have been the most incredible moment with her, and I feel like a schmuck. These questions haunted Korey to the point of regret.

"Can we talk for a moment?" he asks Dr. Fairchild. "Making love to you was beautiful, it was incredible. I told you that I love you."

"And what's the point, Korey?"

"There's no point. Do you love me?"

"Honestly, I don't know what I'm feeling. It was wonderful, but I don't know if my feelings were just for the moment."

"Please don't spare me any words."

"I'm not trying to be mean or to hurt you. You asked.

"Korey, what do you want from me? I can't make you any promises. Can we just enjoy what we have and leave it at that, no expectations?"

"Do you have feelings for me beyond being a colleague?" Korey asks.

"Feelings, yes, I have feelings for you, but I can't say exactly what they are. I don't know what I'm feeling for anyone. It just happened. Please don't make me regret this moment.

"If you want me to commit to something more, I cannot at this time. I'm sorry if I'm not giving you what you want. The sex was beautiful. Thank you," replies Dr. Fairchild.

"You don't have to be so damn arrogant about it. The 'sex'? You make it sound as though I was hired to do a job. Let's keep it business between us. I'm sorry that I thought there was more."

"Would it have made a difference?" Dr. Fairchild asks.

"Yes, I wouldn't have touched you."

Chapter Forty-Eight

It is awkward for Korey, the first few hours working with Dr. Fairchild after their rendezvous. The rejection and her reaction is a double hitter to his ego.

"I have an appointment with Mr. James, the owner of the gas station located next to Paddy's bait shop. At Paddy's funeral, he asked if I plan to sell the bait shop. I told him no, but I've been thinking about it. And why should I let the business go down?" says Dr. Fairchild.

"Interesting!"

"If he is still interested, I will sell the bait shop to him. Don't be so overjoyed."

"Bailey, I think it makes sense to sell it to someone who shows a true interest. What about the gallery?" Korey asks.

"I think I will ship the paintings to a warehouse. I already found a warehouse near downtown Montreal. I am not sure what I want to do with the paintings long term."

"Hey, I'm sorry for the awkwardness. Still friends?"

"When I'm back, I would like to tell you why I left Alabama and quit art school."

"That would be nice. I'll continue to work on Paddy's clues. Do you think you are going to sell the house?"

"I don't think so. At least, not for now."

Dr. Fairchild walks up to a tall, willowy, gruffly looking man. She waits while he finishes pumping gas into an old rusty pickup truck. Mr. James spits tobacco on the ground, leaving a trail to Dr. Fairchild.

"Good morning, Ms. Fairchild. What can I do for ya?"

A man of few words. "I won't take much of your time. Are you still interested in buying the bait shop?"

"Yes."

"Are you sure?"

His smile is so big, you can see between his teeth and the black tartar molded over his gums.

"Is $40,000 agreeable?" Dr. Fairchild asks.

"Oh yes, I can have the money to you by the end of the week," Mr. James confirms.

"Do you know Mr. Clarkson Wade, the attorney?"

"I sure do."

"Meet me in his office this Friday, and we will sign the papers."

Mr. James shakes Dr. Fairchild's hand and gives her a big hug. It pleases Dr. Fairchild to make his wish come true. Mr. James wanted the bait shop for years.

"Korey, I am back."

"How did it go?"

"It went well. I sold the bait shop for $40,000."

"Isn't that low? You probably could have sold it for more."

"Maybe so, but I didn't want the bait shop to sit empty or lose any business. I am not trying to make a killing. It made Mr. James happy. In today's economy, I feel I was lucky to have made the deal that I did."

Dr. Fairchild pours her and Korey a glass of wine.

"Would you like to join me?" she questions as she hands the glass to Korey.

"Sure. What's on your mind? I can tell when there's something you want to discuss."

"I thought this would be a good time to discuss or answer any questions you might have about my secret past."

"Why did you drop out of art school and go into forensics? They are like night and day."

"In high school, my first puppy love was Cameron Jeffries. We talked about getting married once we graduated from college. He wanted to be a police officer, and I wanted to pursue art. Cameron is mix. His mother is Creole and his father is white. Our relationship was sweet and innocent and in the wrong era. As you well know, the South didn't take a liking to any mixed couples. It didn't matter that he was part black. In the South, you were black period. A prominent white girl dating a black boy was taboo. There was a lot of gossiping in town, and it was painful. It was hard for us, but we were so in love."

"Oh, how was Paddy with this?"

"He was the best. Paddy would tell anyone to mind their business and didn't want us to shun from it either. He only emphasized that we be careful and don't flaunt ourselves publicly. He believed that if we kept our respect, so would others. But that was a huge understatement."

"I wish I could have met him. What an icon?"

"Paddy loved Cameron. He told us that our choice to be together would bring heartache, but we had to keep our heads up high.

"I left for art school, and, while I was gone, Cameron joined the police department. He ranked the highest in his class. Oddly enough, the other police officers liked Cameron. And the first year, it was the dream job."

"Why oddly enough?"

"These were the same police officers who were punks in high school that made our lives hell.

"Cameron's mother died shortly after he joined the police academy. The doctors said she had a bad heart. Cameron felt otherwise. He felt it was our relationship, even though she liked me and supported us dating. The people in town were very cruel to her for being Creole. His father left Alabama after her death.

"Cameron was bright and ambitious. He was made detective in less than two years. Then the hell started. They would call him half-breed and wouldn't sit next to him. Their words were harsh and evil. 'You, boy, are still a nigger. You belong at the back of the bus.'"

"Did he complain or try to get anyone to stop them? He was a detective, it's horrible."

"The police chief was an ass. He wouldn't help Cameron. A local black man was killed in the line of duty. That is how his death was written in the local newspaper. He wasn't even acknowledged as a detective."

"How did you find out about Cameron?"

"Paddy called me, frantically. I came home. My first stop was the police department. I asked his superior what happened. His response was they were working on a drug bust that went sour. The police chief ordered Cameron to go as back up in Biloxi, Mississippi, which was out of their jurisdiction, but they were after the drug lords. This was a long overdue bust. Cameron arrived at the scene, and he was alone with no backup. Cameron called for backup. The police chief ordered him to go in and scan the premises. He approached the house and was gunned down by four drug lords. They were paid off and were never arrested."

"It sounds like a setup."

"It was. An officer resigned within days and approached me, confirming everything Cameron said about how they treated him. In so many words, he also confirmed the setup. He said they closed the case and was ordered never to be discussed. He handed me a copy of the report. It was a bloodbath. Only Cameron's blood was shed. The evidence vanished. I know in my heart that there was evidence. Every crime has evidence."

"I am so sorry," says Korey.

"After what happened to Cameron, I decided to quit art school, and I went into forensics. I made a promise to Cameron that there will never be another botched up case. My mission after his death was to be the best in forensics. When I came back to Alabama as a forensic anthropologist, my first case was Cameron's. The police chief was near to retirement. I was determined."

"What was his reaction when you approached him?"

"One could only imagine. He called the district attorney and the judge. He tried everything in his power to stop me. I was unstoppable. It took me less than six months."

"Bailey, I am surprised you weren't scared. You were dealing with ruthless people."

"I was too angry to be scared. Four of the five officers were fired and served time for their conspiracy and second degree murder. The entire department went under investigation. The police chief was forced into an early retirement without his pension. The police department made a statement to the newspaper acknowledging Detective Cameron Jeffries for his heroic response, which caused his death in the line of duty to save his fellow officers. This case is now closed by the FBI."

"The FBI was involved?"

"No. It was their way of saving grace. Being engaged to Cameron was the only time that I came close to being married. The town didn't like me for years. It was just recently that I felt some warmth."

"Why do you think it took so long for the iceberg to thaw?"

"This is a small community. The gossip became their life. For most, it preoccupied them from their miserable lives."

"Do you miss painting?"

"Sometimes. It has been so long that I'm a little intimidated to start painting again."

"I try not to think about that part of my life. It's painful and I am afraid of Pandora's Box. I guess it was best to keep it buried than to deal with the loss. That's probably why I allow myself to be consumed by work. I keep saying I want to semiretire. Maybe I might open a gallery."

"Thanks for sharing a part of you that is so painful. What you have shared makes you more intriguing, a better understanding of your substance as a woman," says Korey. "Were you serious about opening a gallery?"

"Very much so. Paddy was pretty excited and supportive."

"It's obvious. Who has a gallery next to a bait shop?" Korey chuckled.

"It kept Paddy connected to me, and I think he was lonely. I didn't visit him as often as I should have."

"Why Canada?"

"My first job. The medical examiner in Quebec needed an assistant ME. It was perfect for me. Plus, I needed to leave Alabama. A few years of working with the best medical examiners was a great hands-on experience. I was introduced to a brilliant forensic anthropologist. Meeting her sets my new path in life. We worked well together. She's a great teacher. Everything she taught me, I applied to Cameron's case. His botched up investigation made me more determined to be extremely perfect and thorough. There would always be proof without a shadow of a doubt."

"I am a witness to your perfection. It's admirable to be so devoted," says Korey.

"Cameron's death should have never happened, let alone the evidence being tampered with and the police department being corrupted. The police were laundering money from the sale of the drugs they confiscated."

"Do you think, by any chance, that someone from that time may have a vendetta towards you? This revenge could muster enough hate to stir up a serial killer."

"That's a good question. I guess that could be a strong possibility. I never thought about it again after I cleared Cameron's name."

"Bailey, I think we should look into this. I don't recommend we treat this lightly."

"I think anything is possible."

"Were you able to decipher any more clues? What about the evidence from the medical examiner?"

"Still puzzling; the evidence was just the basic routine stuff. They did deliver the stain from the carpet. It was hematemesis."

"Did the report state what caused the blood in the vomit?"

"The convulsion was triggered by the nitroglycerin that induced intense pressure, resulting to the bleeding."

"I requested an analysis on his blood and stomach. I was surprised with the report; it was vague."

"Are you able to work on Paddy's case for a while? I am going to the newspaper and see what articles I can find relating to Cameron's death. Maybe there might be information that could lead us to a suspect. What I can't find at the newspaper, I'll go online. Maybe there's a family member or friend who wants vengeance."

Dr. Fairchild left to pursue her mission. The phone rings. At first, Korey was reluctant to answer. *Maybe it's the medical examiner responding to my request.*

"Hello, Paddy Fairchild's residence. How may I help you?"

No response, silence.

"Hello."

A deep husky voice responds.

"We need to meet immediately," he says.

A little nervous but curious, Korey responds cautiously.

"What is this about? Why the drama?"

"Just meet me at the bait shop, alone. Don't tell Dr. Fairchild. She mustn't know. Don't tell anyone if you want her to stay safe," demands the mystery caller.

"You have more drama than the local playhouse. Why should I meet you?"

"Again, it's recommended strongly if you want to keep Dr. Fairchild out of harm's way."

"What time?"

"Now."

"How will I know who you are?"

"Don't worry I'll find you."

The road to the bait shop is winding. Each curve accentuated Korey's nausea. *Calm down, it's for Bailey.*

He notices that when he pulls into the parking lot, there are no cars; he is alone.

Great, this doesn't look good. I hope this wasn't a wild goose chase.

Korey decides to leave the car, hesitant at first. But now, his curiosity is kicking in. He peeks in the bait shop window. It's dark, no street lights, not even a full moon. There isn't anyone in sight. The mystery has now become unnerving.

He walks around the building. Standing at the end of the alley are two well-dressed men in business suits. One, tall and very lean; the other, short and stocky. The two men walk towards Korey. Simultaneously, they reach in their breast pocket and flash open their FBI badges.

"Sorry for the mystery. It is important that it's handled this way. Did you tell anyone?"

"No."

"Good. I'm Agent Jack Monroe and this is my partner, Agent Ross McQuire. Will you come this way, please?"

Agent Monroe points to the opposite direction.

"There's a black sedan with tinted windows parked behind the bait shop."

The agents escort Korey towards the sedan.

"What's this all about? Why me?"

"We need you to get into the vehicle."

At first Korey resists. He isn't comfortable going into the car, not knowing if Dr. Fairchild is safe.

"Please, sir, get in the vehicle!" the agent yells.

Korey slides onto the black leather seats and bumps into an older nice looking man. The gentleman greets him with a smile that he recognizes from somewhere.

"Do you remember me? I'm Agent Robert Clark. We briefly met during the investigation of Libby Grayson."

"Yes, vaguely. I'm going to ask again, what is this all about? Why not meet me at Paddy Fairchild's house?"

"Dr. Fairchild is in danger. We believe she is in the midst of a serial killer and is being set up as the assailant. The person we are after is very clever and dangerous. You must not tell Dr. Fairchild. It's best she doesn't know at this time for her protection."

"Basically, you're using Dr. Fairchild as bait. No pun intended. I couldn't resist since we are parked in the back of the bait shop."

"I guess you could say that. We don't have any other choice. We seem to always be two steps behind the killer. You're a real wise ass."

"No. I'm pissed at this whole scenario. I don't think you give Dr. Fairchild any credit. This is her expertise. She tracks serial killers. Tell her what is going on and give her around-the-clock protection. You are playing her like she's incompetent."

"I don't mean to come across like we don't have respect for Dr. Fairchild. There's a warrant out for her arrest."

"Arrest for what?"

"For Ms. Grayson's murder."

"Bullshit, she wasn't there."

"Listen, we need you to keep cool. Dr. Fairchild will have to go to Canada to clear herself."

"Christ's sake, she just buried her grandfather. Do you have any empathy? We are trying to solve his murder. His death wasn't accidental."

"I apologize, we didn't know that."

"I thought the feds knew everything, or, at least, they should before they scare the shit out of people. What's my part in this charade?" Korey asks.

"Getting Dr. Fairchild to Canada."

"Why would I do that? I know she is innocent."

"As you so bluntly stated, she is the bait to flush out the killer. This way, we are in control of the situation for their capture."

"The Montreal police department has been informed by us that we need to have hard evidence against Dr. Fairchild. And that we don't have. She has to do the formalities. The warrant is in motion, and we can't stop it."

"We need your cooperation, your word that you will not discuss this meeting with anyone."

The black sedan pulls up next to Korey's car. The FBI agent leans across Korey and opens his door. There were no words exchanged. Dazed and confused, Korey puts his car into drive. The ride back to Paddy's is a blur. *How do I convince Bailey to turn herself in and convey the urgency without arising any suspicion?*

Chapter Forty-Nine

"How was your day? Did you get a lot done on the puzzling clues?"

"My day was interesting. Not much was accomplished regarding the case. I did some research as well."

"Well, I struck out. It seems that every newspaper article and any reports relating to Cameron's case are gone. The six hours wasn't a total waste of time. There was an interesting piece of information from the police chief's retired secretary. She said there's a police report on his daughter that was sealed, marked closed, and filed by her."

"Would you like a glass of wine? Please go on."

"Yes. In the report, the police chief's daughter was seen by a fellow officer with a light-colored Negro necking in a car. In Alabama, it's against the law for any public display of any sexual advances. This incident happened the night before Cameron was killed. This was the date on the report. The Negro was not identified in the report. On the back of the report, it stated CASE CLOSED. The Negro was identified as Cameron Jeffries. It was dated the day of the shooting."

"So, if I understand this. They didn't know who the Negro was with his daughter. Cameron was killed in the line of duty as a cover-up."

"Yes, it was planned and executed by the police chief. He made sure it was buried. It was the most embarrassing act his daughter could have done, let alone being with a Negro."

"This would eliminate any vengeance towards you."

"It doesn't change how I feel about what I did years ago. I still was able to expose the corruption and drug trafficking within the department. Knowing what really happened confirms how horrible the police department was back then."

"Why do you think, after all these years, his secretary decided to tell the tale?"

"Maybe guilt. She said she liked Cameron."

"Your day sounds more productive than mine," states Korey.

"You seem preoccupied. Are you all right?"

"I'm okay. I did get a call from the Montreal police. They need you to come in."

It's best to be frank, no games.

"You make it sound like I'm a fugitive."

"Well, if you don't go willingly, there is a warrant for your arrest. They want to talk to you about Libby."

"I wasn't there."

"I know. It's better if you go sooner than later."

"I'll fly out tomorrow. Will you go with me?"

"If that's what you want. I could stay here and pack up some things at the bait shop and the gallery."

"You're right. Mr. James would like to take over this week. The paintings, ship to the warehouse in Montreal. Everything in the house will stay; cover the furniture. The Model T Ford, leave in the garage. Please be sure to cover it well. Eventually, I will have it transported to the warehouse."

"This shouldn't take more than a few days. Dr. Kendall is planning to continue with Paddy's case. I'll meet with her when I am done."

"I am calling it a night. Sleep well. I'll see you in the morning before I leave."

"Good night."

I am so tired. I can't sleep. Why am I seeing Libby and Perry together every time I close my eyes? Please, God, forgive me.

Chapter Fifty

"Call me when you arrive. Appease me."

"I will. Don't worry about me."

"Any other time I wouldn't, but there's a killer out there and you are marked as their prey."

"You're right."

Dr. Fairchild tried to relax during the flight. She spent more time looking over her shoulder. Everyone was a suspect, especially women. After her last encounter in flight, Dr. Fairchild scoped the plane for any large floppy hats. At this flight, she made a point to stay awake.

"Hey, beautiful, sorry I'm late. The traffic was a mess," explains Perry.

"It's okay, I didn't wait long. My luggage seems to have taken another route. Never mind, it's now coming around."

"Something weird just happened. I could have sworn I saw you on the other side of the airport."

"What do you mean?"

"Just what I said, there's someone who looks like you."

"Here, grab my luggage, please. Show me where you saw her."

"Bailey, I am sure it's nothing to be alarmed about. It's an honest mistake. It happens all the time."

"Perry, look outside. The woman going into the cab, is that her?" Dr. Fairchild asks frantically.

"Yes, I think so."

"Why are we running?" Perry asks.

"I want to follow that cab."

The cab driver picks up Dr. Fairchild's luggage.

"Please, can you hurry?" demands Dr. Fairchild.

"Calm down. You don't have to be rude," says Perry.

"Damn, it's too late. They're gone."

"Please take me to the Montreal police department."

"You mean us."

"No, I'll meet you at your office when I am done."

"Would you please explain to me what this last episode was all about?" Perry asks.

"Not now, I will later."

"Are you sure you don't want me to go? A lot has happened while you were gone."

"I'll be fine. I'm a big girl."

"A stubborn one that's for sure."

"If you don't mind, I will get my luggage later at your office."

"Thanks for the ride." Dr. Fairchild hands the driver the fare and smiles at Perry while exiting the cab.

"See you later," says Dr. Fairchild.

***

"Hello. May I please see the chief of police?"

"May I tell him who's here to see him?"

"Your name, Miss?" the officer asks.

"I am Dr. Bailey Fairchild."

"Oh yes, he is expecting you. He will be glad to see you."

"Please sign the register." He pushes the book gently towards her.

"Good afternoon, Dr. Fairchild. I am Police Chief Francois Roux. Please follow me."

"Have a seat." He points to a brown leather chair that is placed in front of his cherry red desk.

"I'm going to get right to the point. You're a person of interest in the murder of Libby Grayson."

"She was my assistant and friend. Please don't make it sound as though she was an enemy."

"That's not how I meant it to come across."

He lines numerous photos in front of Dr. Fairchild on the desk.

"You can see, Dr. Fairchild, by the photos of the crime scene why you are a suspect. Your DNA and fingerprints were found on the window of the vehicle where her body was mutilated."

"I understand all of this, but there is one very important fact that proves I didn't commit this crime. I was in Atlantic City at the time of her death."

"Do you have an alibi?"

"Yes. You can call Dr. Katherine Kendall. I was working on a case with her."

"There's also the murder of Inspector LaFleur. He was found dead in a hotel room in Alabama. Inspector LaFleur has been following you since the attack in your home."

"That was some time ago. I didn't report the incident." Dr. Fairchild's voice raises a few octaves.

"I know. Ms. Grayson did after you left for Atlantic City."

"Can you explain to me why it was Inspector LaFleur I saw standing at my feet as I was passing out?"

"That wasn't mentioned in his report."

"I wonder why. Why was the inspector always in the shadow of my cases? What was his obsession with me?

"There was a foreboding presence. You could call it a gut feeling, intuition. And he always leaves his calling card: gross cigar butts. I'd say his work habits were pretty sloppy from such a thorough inspector."

"Read this letter that was addressed to the inspector. This will explain what may have seemed to be an obsession."

The chief of police hands Dr. Fairchild a plastic bag. The only content is the letter.

Mr. Inspector,

I strongly urge you to have Dr. Fairchild back off from the case she is working on in Atlantic City, if you don't want your niece to end up dead like the body that was found in the cranberry bogs. This is no warning, it's a promise.

The letter was typed on a brown paper bag.

"The inspector received the letter the morning of your attack. He was planning to visit you. What he didn't expect is how he found you."

"You said earlier that Libby called in the incident."

"She did after the fact. Surprisingly, the inspector doesn't have a niece. That is why he kept it a secret even from the department."

"This sounds a bit peculiar."

"He didn't want the person who wrote the letter to know that he didn't have a niece. While he was trying to protect someone in the department, he was trying to find out who was after you."

"Did the inspector ever find out whose niece was threatened?"

"Yes. She is my niece, my sister's only child."

"Were there any fingerprints?"

"No. The plastic bag wasn't unusual. Every store carries this brand."

"Would you mind if my forensic team ran tests on the evidence that you do have?"

"That would be fine."

"Do you honestly believe that I killed Libby?"

"No."

"Then why am I here?"

"I was hoping you would help us find who killed Inspector LaFleur. And I do believe you are in danger."

"I have assigned two of my best inspectors to watch you around the clock."

"Thank you. That won't be necessary. For me to work efficiently, they would only be in the way."

"Dr. Fairchild…"

"Please call me Bailey."

"Bailey, you do realize what you are doing by saying no. You are putting yourself in such a high exposure with no protection from the killer."

"I appreciate your thoughtfulness, but this is the only way. I am very sorry about the inspector. I will help you."

The police chief stares at Dr. Fairchild for a moment and smiles. He tries to hold back his concern, the fear that her life is in jeopardy.

He genuinely is concern for my safety. This is serious; his face wears roads of stress.

"Police Chief Roux. I would be able to work with the inspectors if they don't crowd me. They could surveillance the outside of my house. Please, just emphasize to them not to breathe down my neck."

"Thank you. That's agreeable, if you will call me Hector. They are outside in the hall, waiting to start their first surveillance." He smiles with relief.

"Police Chief Roux, may I go or do I need to be interrogated?"

"We are done. Where should I send the evidence for testing?"

"Dr. Katherine Kendall. She is the medical examiner in Atlantic City. I'll tell her to put a rush on this. May I review Inspector LaFleur's report?"

"Actually, I'll send them with the evidence to Dr. Kendall."

Dr. Fairchild shakes the police chief's hand.

"Hector, I'll be in touch. Oh, who handled Libby's investigation?"

"The inspector. I will include that report with the other documents going to Dr. Kendall."

"Who knows about the letter?"

"Only you, the inspector, and me."

"Thank you."

"Do you need a ride? Your condo is still under investigation. You will have to stay somewhere else."

"I am getting used to hotels."

"I will have one of the detectives drop you off."

"Detective Murphy this is Dr. Fairchild. Please take her to wherever she needs to go. Important: make sure she isn't being followed."

"Where am I taking you?"

"The district attorney's office on Kingston."

"That's just a few blocks from here. The police chief is very concerned for your safety. He might be a little pushy, but his intentions are meaningful."

"Here we are. The building is dark. Would you like me to escort you in?"

"I'll be fine. I am meeting a DA. Thank you for the ride. Good night."

Dr. Fairchild is surprised. There are no lights visible from outside. It's been six hours since she parted from Perry. Usually, the main door to the building is locked. Dr. Fairchild would have called Perry, but her cell is in the pocket of her luggage. The lobby area is dark. A clanging noise disrupts the silence. It's the cleaning crew. There are footsteps in unison with the clanging cart. She's unable to see who is walking at the end of the corridor. Dr. Fairchild hides behind the receptionist's station. The footsteps stop; the atmosphere reverts to silence.

Take a deep breath, girl, and relax. It's only the cleaning staff.

The ride on the elevator is eerie. Any other time, she would have taken the stairs. Her discussion earlier with the police chief that her life is in danger causes fear to host deeply within her soul.

Every noise and movement has Dr. Fairchild on the edge. Standing in the elevator alone intensifies the fear. The elevator stops on the sixth floor.

"Hello, is anyone there?"

No response. Dr. Fairchild stands in the doorway, looking around the very dark opening, too scared to step out. She steps back into the center of the elevator. Before the door closes, half of a body charges in, trying to keep the doors from closing. Dr. Fairchild screams that her chest hurts with every breath, paralyzed from fear. The body turns towards Dr. Fairchild.

"Bailey! Oh, my God, I am so sorry to have frightened you."

"Shit, Perry." She punches his chest with her fist.

"I just about died of a heart attack."

"What are you doing down here?" inquired Perry.

"I called out. There was no answer."

"I came here for a soda," he says.

He puts the ice-cold soda can on her face.

"Only the sixth floor has soda machines."

"Funny," she says as she pushes his hand away."

"So, how was the interrogation? I was getting a little worried you were detained for a long time."

The only light glimmering on the eighth floor was peering beneath the doorway into Perry's office.

"It went pretty well. I'll tell you all about it over dinner. I am starving."

"My treat since I scared the crap out of you," offers Perry. "We'll go after I lock up."

"What happened here?" Dr. Fairchild asks.

"I don't know. I was only gone a half hour tops. It looks like a bomb went off," he states.

"Is anything missing?"

"It doesn't seem so. Only the papers that I was working on are scattered everywhere."

"Perry, look at the filing cabinet. There is a drawer that's not completely closed."

"One guess of what file has been taken?"

"I don't know," Dr. Fairchild replies.

"Why were you asked to come back?"

"Libby?"

"That's the one!"

"I am calling the police chief."

Within ten minutes, the building looks like a police convention. There are officers in Perry's office dusting for fingerprints. They are like bees on honey in the elevator, scanning the stairway.

"Police Chief, I am surprised to see you here."

"I told you I would have the protection you needed. I granted your request. The police officers are well hidden, but visible when warranted."

"I am impressed. Thank you."

"You two can leave. We will lock up when we are done. Try and have a good evening," says the police chief.

"It's pretty late. I don't know of any place that serves after ten o'clock," says Perry.

"I do. Schwartz Deli. He has the best tourtières. It would be wonderful to see him."

"Tourt a whom?"

"You live in Canada and you haven't had a tourtière?"

"I have a rule of thumb: if I can't say the damn thing, I usually don't eat it."

"This is a real treat."

"Okay, you have my curiosity."

Dr. Fairchild gives Perry the directions. She dozes off instantly as soon as the car is in motion.

"Hey, beautiful, we are here?"

Perry hands Dr. Fairchild his handkerchief.

"You might want to wipe the drool from your mouth."

"I am hungry. I've only had coffee all day."

"Before we go in, what is a tourtière?"

"Originated from Quebec, it is a meat pie served at Christmas. Schwartz Deli is the only deli around that serves the tourtière year-round. It's filled with meat, most commonly pork and onions."

"Hmmm…mouthwatering. Will he be open?"

"Paulo is always opened."

They stand outside the deli and knock a few times on the door and window.

"Paulo, it is Bailey."

He opens the door abruptly, swings it widely open, and charges towards Dr. Fairchild. He grabs her and embraces with no intentions of letting her go.

"Bailey, my dear, it's been so long. How are you? You're gorgeous as always, my sunshine," he rattles off in his strong French accent.

"Paulo, I am wonderful. I apologize that it's late. We haven't eaten all day, and I have been boasting about your tourtière."

"Please come in, sit down. I'll get Mama. We'll get you supper right away."

"Mama, it's Bailey. She is here with a friend. Get the best wine on your way down."

"This is quaint. He is a character."

"Paulo and his wife have run this business for over forty years. They treat me like a daughter."

"Do they have children?"

"No."

"You can tell he adores you."

"Hello, Bailey, dear. Glad to see you. Who is your handsome friend?"

"This is Perry Sinclair. He is the district attorney in Montreal. We are working on a case."

"We read in the newspapers about your assistant, Libby. Is that the case you're working on?"

"Yes."

"We won't bother you, so you may have alone time like love birds should have."

"Did I hear her correctly, 'love birds'?"

"Yes. Paulo and Mama are always trying to get me to settle down."

"What is Mama's name? I would like to address her appropriately."

"I've only known her as Mama. I don't know her first name. They're last name is Schwartz. They don't want to be addressed as Mr. or Mrs. Schwartz, just Paulo and Mama."

"May I pour you a glass of Georges Duboeuf. This wine is made from the gamay grapes from the French province of Beaujolais. The light-bodied red wine has a spicy flavor with an aroma of peach."

"Perfect. It sounds delightful."

"He knows his wines. They are like his children."

"When Paulo says his 'best,' this is the best. It tangos well with the tourtière."

Perry smells the aroma escaping from the wine glass. His mouth aches with the anticipation to combine the two zealous flavors of food and wine.

"I can smell the pork and onions. If it smells this heavenly, I can only imagine what the flavor will do to my taste buds."

Perry's first bite is enchanting.

"You are absolutely correct. The combination of this to-die-for dish and this incredible wine is dancing the tango with every savory bite.

"You won't be offended if I continue to get lost into my world of food bliss?"

"No, I am already there."

Their supper is more than incredible. They indulge into the tourtière and the wine. Not a word has been spoken.

"Paulo, thank you for a spectacular supper. It was a pleasure as always to see you and Mama."

"You are welcome. Come back more often. We miss you. Be safe. Mr. Sinclair, please take extra care of our Bailey."

"No worries. Thanks. The tourtière was delightful. I'll definitely be back."

Perry drives up to the valet to drop Dr. Fairchild off at the hotel. Dr. Fairchild pauses and looks at Perry, hesitant to open the car door.

"I am sorry about Libby. You know you were getting close."

"In the beginning, we were. But she turned out to be a royal pain in the ass."

"She didn't deserve what happened to her."

"I agree. She portrayed you and this is what she unintentionally brought upon herself."

"Why is it you keep staring at me?"

"I have a favor to ask, as if you haven't done enough already. Would you please stay the night? Strictly for company; no funny business. I don't mean to come across as though I am using you."

"I wasn't thinking that. Despite everything we have been through, I am a nice guy."

"Perry, I am scared, really scared."

"I know. I would be honor to."

"Excuse me, would you please park the car?" Perry asks the valet attendant.

Perry grabs Dr. Fairchild's luggage from the backseat and looks around. He is a little nervous himself. He felt some reassurance when he observed the parked police car across the street.

"Hello, Dr. Fairchild," says the police officer in the lobby.

"Good evening," replies Dr. Fairchild.

"Good morning, how may I help you?" the reservation clerk asks.

"Oh, it is morning."

"My key, please. I am Dr. Fairchild. What type of room do I have?"

"You have a room with a king-size bed."

"Would it be possible to get a room with a suite?

"I'll check. We have a suite with a Jacuzzi and two queen-size beds on the twelfth floor."

"Perfect."

"You really don't trust me."

"Did you ever stop and think I may not trust myself?" Dr. Fairchild smiles suggestively.

"Any luck in finding Mousey?"

"A neighbor on your block approached me when I went with the police to examine your condo for evidence. She didn't have Mousey at the time, but she said she thought Mousey was roaming in her yard."

"Would you like to spend tomorrow looking for her? We could go to the animal shelters and check with local vets."

"That sounds good."

"Perry, look, there's already a police officer planted next to my room. They don't waste any time."

"That's relieving. The police chief called me, after you left his office, confirming he would have you watched like a hawk. And he meant it."

"Good morning, Dr. Fairchild and Mr. Sinclair," says the police officer.

"Good morning. Me staying here might tarnish your image," says Perry.

"I think under these circumstances, they understand."

"Do you want a night cap? The bar is loaded."

"No, thanks, I am going to bed. Thank you for a lovely evening. I had fun," says Dr. Fairchild.

"Help yourself to anything."

"I already have sweet dreams. See you in the morning."

Perry's normal reaction would be to use his boyish charms to seduce Dr. Fairchild. For the first time, he is putting Dr. Fairchild's emotional needs before his selfish desires.

Chapter Fifty-One

"Hello, are you Mr. James?"

"Yes, how may I help you?"

"I am Korey, a friend of Dr. Fairchild. I will be packing up the paintings and shipping them out today. Are you going to keep the name Fishing Art?"

"Of course, Paddy kept a selection of Dr. Fairchild's work and paintings of people fishing. He drew in the crowd. The paintings are impressive. How is Dr. Fairchild doing, you know, with all that has been happening?"

"She's doing all right, considering."

"She was very close to her grandfather. I knew him for many years, nice guy. I remember when she had pig tails and a puny little thing. Let me know if there is anything you need or if I can help in anyway," offers Mr. James.

There are thirty or more paintings in the gallery. *Mr. James is correct. The selection is impressive.*

Korey has his favorites: the Mona Lisa and a few of the paintings that were of people fishing. *Quite clever. I see where Bailey gets some of her creativity.*

Korey decides to have the paintings from Paddy's house delivered to the gallery. He thinks it would be easier to have one location for a pickup. The guys he hires to haul the paintings are determined to take their time. It is getting late in the day.

"Sir, we are not going to be able to bring over these two crates across the ferry to Dauphin Island. The last ferry out is at four o'clock, and it's after four," says the mover.

"Can you be back tomorrow morning? I am on a deadline and need to ship to Montreal by the end of the week."

"Sure, we will be here at ten. We don't start any earlier," he replies.

"If I pay you an extra hundred dollars, can you be here at eight?" Korey pleads.

"No, sir, ten is the earliest."

"Okay, until ten tomorrow." *I shouldn't be so surprised.*

Korey locks up the bait shop and proceeds over to the gas station.

"Mr. James, I have to finish tomorrow. I thought I would have the paintings removed today. The movers have a set time frame, not very many working hours."

"No problem. We on Dauphin Island have a different lifestyle everything is done; leisurely."

"I am going to miss Paddy and Dr. Fairchild."

"Tell Dr. Fairchild I am sorry I didn't go over and say good-bye when she was here the other day."

Korey starts to walk away until he realizes what Mr. James said.

"When did you say Dr. Fairchild was here?"

"Well, let me think. I was putting water in a customer's car when I glanced over. She was peeking in the windows. I thought it was odd in all."

"What day? When?"

"Ummm…"

"It's important you remember."

Korey is agitated and demanding.

"The other day, just before dusk. She didn't stay long. Dr. Fairchild always wore those big hats that flop around. They're kind of funny looking."

"Did you see her face?"

"No, I guess not. Just that big hat. You don't have to be so pushy or rude. I thought it was her," Mr. James sighs.

"I am sorry. You did fine. I will see you tomorrow."

There is no way that was Bailey. Korey replays his conversation with Mr. James in his mind. *Bailey was with me getting ready for her trip to Canada. This doesn't make sense.*

Korey doesn't realize how many paintings are in Paddy's garage. There are at least forty. He stops counting and decides to call Dr. Fairchild. He goes straight to her voicemail. He calls Perry's office and leaves a message with his receptionist to call.

"Hello."

"Good morning, Korey. I just got your message. The cell phone was in my luggage."

"I was concerned. I didn't hear from you since you left yesterday morning."

"I was detained at the police headquarters for hours. I went to dinner with Perry. We didn't get back to the hotel until late."

"That sounds cozy."

"It's not what you think. There was an incident in his office. I didn't want to be alone."

"Mr. James said he saw you poking around the bait shop the other night."

"We know that's impossible. I was with you."

"I know."

"How can he be so sure it was me?"

"The big picture hat that he thought you were wearing."

Dr. Fairchild's heart pounds rapidly, pumping faster and faster. She has become silent.

"Bailey, Bailey, are you there?"

"Yes," she replies, barely able to speak. Fear has settled as a lump in her throat.

"Who the hell is this mystery person?" Korey asks.

"I don't know. You said person not a woman."

"Are we sure it's a woman? Our evidence is circumstantial according to Paddy's ridiculous clues," states Korey.

"Excuse me. I don't need your condescending statements. What's not circumstantial is the fact that there's a serial killer at large. Whether it is a man or woman, I am their target."

"Are there police protecting you?"

"Yes, there is an officer in the lobby. They follow me everywhere, and Perry is here, too."

"And let's not forget Perry being the white knight."

"Korey, your juvenile behavior towards Perry is unacceptable. I have to go."

"Bailey, wait. I was wrong for barking about Perry being there. It isn't professional or mature."

"Fine, how's the packing coming along?"

"There are three crates with about ten paintings each that are still at the bait shop. I will be working on the paintings in Paddy's garage tomorrow. He has quite the collection."

"They are not all mine. He does have the collection. He loved art."

"I found a painting by you, one of my favorites. A man and a child were sitting and dangling their feet over the edge of the pier, fishing."

"That was Paddy and me. I painted it when I was in high school."

"I will have the rest of the paintings crated and ready to ship by tomorrow."

"Excellent. Do your best to finish up tomorrow. I do appreciate everything you are doing. When this project is done, I need you to assist Dr. Kendall."

"What's going on?"

"I have asked the police chief to send the inspector's reports to Dr. Kendal. I will be working with Perry on Libby's case.

"With the cases that we are working on, it will be best to split them. I believe that they are connected to what have been happening, the murders and the stalking of me."

"I will leave for Atlantic City tomorrow evening.
Stay safe, bye," says Korey.

Even though Perry is with Dr. Fairchild for protection, Korey is having a hard time trusting Perry alone with Dr. Fairchild. He knows their history and Dr. Fairchild always gives in to Perry's charm. Perry walks over to Bailey.

"You look troubled." Says Perry.

"Korey said that Mr. James saw a woman peeking in the window of the bait shop."

"Who is Mr. James?"

"He is the man who bought Paddy's bait shop."

"What's the problem?"

"Mr. James said he thought it was me. It's the night when I was with Korey. She dressed like me, with the big floppy hat."

"Like the woman I saw at the airport."

"Exactly. Korey will be working with Dr. Kendall on the inspector's case.

"Can we leave soon to investigate the whereabouts of Mousey? This will be my last attempt. I am behind the eight ball, and I need to get into my work mind."

"I am ready anytime."

"I have an appointment to meet with the medical examiner this afternoon."

"Keep in mind how difficult this will be for you to review," states Perry.

"Libby's murder is the key to three killings. I have to prove it. They intertwine with me and why I am a target."

"Her death was very violent. Will you be able to handle it?"

"Are you questioning my ability as a forensic anthropologist?"

"No. You are human, and this is very close to you."

"This will no doubt be one of my more difficult cases. I realize that if her killer has anything to do with Paddy and the inspector's death, I have a serial killer after me. Confirming this makes it more frightening."

"For me, anyone wanting me dead would be frightening. Is there a difference?" Perry asks.

"Yes. To a serial killer, it's more personal."

"I would think wanting me dead is personal," says Perry.

"What I mean or I should have said is it's more of a game. They enjoy the thrill of watching their victims squirm like a cat and mouse game. It's not enough to just kill the person. They get a personal satisfaction by harming the closest to the victim, a form of torture before the serial killer devours their prey. It is hard to track them down. You have to go into the serial killers' minds to understand what makes them tick."

"Please don't take any chances. Stay in the officers' view at all times. I don't want you to become their next victim."

"That's why I have to know these serial killers' minds, how they think, so I would know how to approach. I don't want anyone to become a victim either because of me. I have to be thorough to get a conviction. I didn't protect Paddy."

"How could you have known?" Perry asks. "Do you have any idea who killed him? No, you don't. So stop blaming yourself for his death. It's ridiculous."

"We both have a lot to do. I will see you later," Dr. Fairchild states.

"Would you like to meet up for dinner?"

"Honestly, I don't know if that would be a good idea."

"You have to eat. I promise I'll be a good boy," says Perry.

"I will think about it. It will depend on my meeting with the medical examiner. I will call you later."

Dr. Fairchild arrives at the medical examiner's office before hours.

"Thanks for meeting me so early. I would like to go over Libby Grayson's autopsy report."

"It's no problem."

"Going forward, I will be addressing Ms. Grayson as the victim.

"The report states that the victim's forehead was bashed. The cranium was visible from a deep and wide gash. The trauma to the head was caused by the force from continuous bashing against the steering wheel. There were multiple abrasions across the victim's face.

"It was quite a bloody, gruesome crime scene. We collected chunks of her cranium, with hair sticking on the steering wheel, as well as the window," states the medical examiner.

"There were scratches on the right cheek bone, approximately two inches in length down to the jaw line. The scratches were determined as being inflected by an animal, a feline."

Mousey must have been terrified. The ordeal was horrendous. She hated being in the car. The adventure going to the vet was a traumatic experience by itself. If Libby wasn't dead, I would have been livid for putting Mousey in this unnecessary drama and wrecking my classic car.

Libby's life, being terminated, didn't seem to affect Bailey as much as one would think. Libby was manipulative, an opportunist, gregarious to the point of being obnoxious. *I won't miss her. These aren't professional thoughts. These are personal.*

"We had a difficult time retrieving any DNA from the car. In fact, it's quite brilliant on the killer's part. The car wash removed most of the evidence."

"How did you know there was a feline in the car?"

"There was animal vomit on the floor mat. The car wash was still spraying water and soap suds when the police arrived."

"The outside of the car was clean of any fingerprints, except for yours, Dr. Fairchild. Your fingerprints were on the windows and under the door handle knob. Do you have an explanation?"

"The most obvious. The damn thing is mine. I am surprised that more of my DNA wasn't found throughout the car."

Dr. Fairchild continues to read the autopsy. Victim was identified by dental records and confirmation of identity by District Attorney Perry Sinclair. The victim is Libby Grayson not Dr. Bailey Fairchild.

"You thought the victim was me?"

"It wasn't me. When I arrived at the crime scene, District Attorney Perry Sinclair was giving his statement to the detective. I didn't get a chance to talk to him. At first, Mr. Sinclair thought it was you for obvious reasons. She was found in your car, wearing your clothes, and her ID was yours. She had fake IDs including a driver's license with your picture? Yes, Libby was determined to be you."

"It states the victim had marks on her throat. May I see the pictures, please? Did they find what was used to make these marks?"

The medical examiner pushes towards Dr. Fairchild a clear sealed envelope.

"That's my scarf. My initials are embroidered on the bottom left of each panel."

"Strangling her was overkill. It was more of a message for me," Dr. Fairchild states.

"I don't think Libby knew what hit her. Literally, the attack was fast and furious. When I arrived at the scene, there were blood splatters throughout the interior of the car. Pieces of the victim's face and hair were posted on the dashboard and windshield. There were pieces of her skull on the interior roof of the car. The killer was angry with a vengeance. There was a lot of rage that fueled this murder," says the medical examiner. "This must be hard for you. I understand she was a friend."

"She was more than a friend. She was my personal assistant as well. We worked many years together. It was a horrible way to die. No one deserves this, especially Libby. What's more disturbing is she was pregnant—a double homicide."

This is the first time that Dr. Fairchild addressed the corpse as "Libby" and not a "victim." She is trying to keep it from being personal, unable to control the situation and her mixed feelings.

"There is evidence that the killer is a woman. The floor mat behind the driver's seat had impressions of high heels."

"I read the report. It stated that the assailant broke the window and grabbed her head, forcing the impact into the steering wheel."

"That's true. Furthermore, in the report, the car door was open and the seat was pushed forward, meaning she climbed into the backseat area and strangled her with the scarf. This was a stupid move for the killer. And this was luck for us. It confirms Ms. Grayson's killer's gender."

"It is evident that the killer was more determined to get a message across than to clean her tracks."

"Thank you for letting me review and analyze the report of the autopsy findings."

"Let me know if there is anything else that I can assist you with."

"I will. I am going to visit the police chief and see if he has any leads on the killer. It's been a month since Libby's death. There has to be something concrete."

The coroner's report is troubling and confusing for Dr. Fairchild. It is disturbing for her to read the graphic details of Libby's death. *She made me angry from all of her betrayal and deceit. Still, nothing can justify the barbaric way she was killed.*

Dr. Fairchild's anger has shifted from Libby to Perry. Perry's blasé attitude towards their relationship and Libby's death has disgusted Dr. Fairchild. *I can't stomach the thought of seeing or talking to Perry anymore.*

This has been a turning point in her life. She has finally released her hypnotic hold with Perry.

"Hello, hello?" Perry asks.

"Hi, it's Bailey. I've decided that I'll pass on the dinner invitation for tonight."

"Do you want a rain check?"

147

"No. No dinner invitation tonight or any other time."

"What's going on?" Perry asks.

"I have spent most of my day with the medical examiner."

"You sound angry."

"Not only angry, I am disgusted."

"With the case?" retorted Perry.

"No, with you."

"Excuse me? Where's this going?"

"I read Libby's autopsy, a horrible barbaric death. She was so desperate to win your love, attention, recognition, or however you want to define it. She felt that the only way to hook you was to portray me. Even to the point of sleeping with you and getting pregnant.

"For the first time, in all the years that we have been friends and lovers, I can truthfully state that I am done with you. Please stay away from me. I frankly don't know how you can stand yourself; no remorse."

"You act as though I killed her, that I had some part in her death."

"Didn't you think about it?"

"Bailey, please, can we talk about this? I thought we came a long way since our dating days and have become better friends."

"I thought so, too, until now. Libby paid a high price. It cost her life, and you are not worth it.

"Please answer my next question honestly. Did you know she was pregnant before she was murdered?"

"Why must you torture yourself? No matter how I answer the question, you will think I am a monster."

"The answer Perry, stop the dancing around the bush routine."

"Yes, I knew. We had a nasty fight the night before she was killed, and I was appalled with her obsession over you. You and I had this discussion, or, should I say, I tried to talk to you weeks ago about this. You so eloquently blew me off. I didn't want to have a child with her. We didn't discuss what we were going to do. She went into a rage and that was the last conversation we had. I am sorry. What happened to Libby was borderline crazy, and I tried to get out of the relationship before she got pregnant."

"You didn't mind screwing her until the end."

"I wasn't thinking. It looks awful. I'm not a monster. It was a mistake."

"I have a meeting with the police chief. Good-bye."

Surprisingly, for Dr. Fairchild, disengaging from Perry came easier than she thought. A sense of relief has given her the strength to move beyond the web of deceit that has kept them entwined for too many years.

Chapter Fifty-Two

"Good afternoon, Dr. Fairchild, I must say your outfit is stunning. I like the bright yellow dress with the white polka dots. It's refreshing to see a woman dress with class and sophistication. You have accented your attire with a striking white floppy hat. I can't tell you the last time I saw a classy well-dressed lady. Years ago, my wife used to wear gloves, nice touch," states the police chief. He was wiping back his drool.

"Thank you for noticing. It's not every day that a man compliments with explicit taste."

What the police chief doesn't know is that Dr. Fairchild has a motive for the outfit, a new beginning for herself. Being attractive to men is her medicine, along with her strength, to overcome her vulnerability with Perry. *I'm impressed the police chief can recognize style.*

"There is something that I didn't send to Dr. Kendall. I have the inspector's notebook. I think you should read it. There's detailed information regarding all the cases that you are working on."

"My cases?" she asks.

"Trust me, please read it. You will find answers to your questions. He states his suspicions of someone stalking you."

"Does he identify the stalker?"

"No, only the gender. The inspector figured out who the killer is but didn't get a chance to let anyone know. It cost him his life.

"I want this case solved. Whatever you need, if it's more officers, let me know."

"I promise I will. I am grateful that you trust that I am innocent."

"Until you prove otherwise, you will stay as a person of interest. Dr. Fairchild, before you leave, I have a question."

"Please, police chief, continue. You have my interest."

"Is it true that you are planning to open a gallery in Quebec?"

"Boy, that spread fast."

"Rumors run like wildfire, especially when it comes to adding culture to our community."

"Yes, I am tossing the idea around, but not in Quebec. I am hoping to find a place in Montreal."

"Well, the best to you."

"You will be on the invitation list for the grand opening when it turns into fruition."

"I would be there anyway to keep an eye on you," replies the police chief in a rude tone.

"I better be going. Again, thank you." *That was an interesting rude encounter.*

His sarcasm leaves a nasty taste in her mouth. Intrigued by the contents in the inspector's notebook, Dr. Fairchild decides this would be the best time to go back to the hotel and divulge herself into the notebook.

"Hello, this is room service. How may I help you?"

"This is Dr. Fairchild in 1212. I would like to order a Cobb salad, please no bacon, and an iced tea with lemon. When will it be delivered?"

"That will be delivered in half an hour."

"Thank you, I will see you then."

Dr. Fairchild reaches for her cell phone that is vibrating across the table.

"This is Dr. Fairchild."

"Hi, gorgeous," says Korey.

"Hello, Korey, nice to hear your voice. How are you?"

"Fine, I am with Dr. Kendall. I just arrived."

"I have shipped all the crates to the warehouse in Montreal, except the Model T Ford. It's covered and secured in Paddy's garage."

"You have done plenty. I will transport the car later. Thanks, I owe you at least a dinner.

"That's a date."

"How is Dr. Kendall?"

"She's great. I understand why the two of you work well together. She has the same ambition, dedication, and standards like you do. Dr.

Kendall has been working on the evidence that was sent by the police chief on the inspector."

"Is there anything that I should know about now?"

"Not really. She had a good idea that the three of us meet and compare all our notes. The cases all interrelate to one another. When we find the connection, we will have our conviction."

"I like the idea. Give me a couple of days. I am working on something here that needs my full attention."

"Should we plan to meet in Montreal this weekend?"

"Yes, that's fine. I will make hotel reservations for Dr. Kendall at the hotel where I am staying. There is a private conference room we can ask for reservation. Everything that we need is conveniently located in the hotel."

"Sounds good. We will see you this weekend. I will tell Dr. Kendall about the hotel room."

"I have to go. I have room service at the door. We'll talk soon."

Dr. Fairchild hangs up and looks through the peephole to confirm if it's room service.

"Please come in. It's such a beautiful evening. Would you please set the tray outside on the table on the veranda?"

The room service attendant stumbles over the leg on the table. He loses his balance and leans into the rail. The rail starts to give way. He grabs for Dr. Fairchild. She pulls him towards her, away from the wobbly rail.

"Are you all right?" She readjusts his coat so each side aligns evenly.

"Yes, ma'am. Thank you."

"Amazing you didn't fall. What's incredible is you didn't spill a drop or let go of the tray."

"I was scared. That would have been a nasty fall."

His stomach gets queasy when he looks down in disbelief that he didn't fall. The service attendant moves his right hand from his forehead to his breast and from the left shoulder to the right in gesture of the sign of the cross. "Oh, Holy Mother of Jesus, thank you," says the service attendant.

"I am glad you are okay." She pays the bill and leaves an extra large tip.

"I will call the front desk to have maintenance repair on the rail immediately."

Dr. Fairchild escorts the attendant to the door. She is feeling a little shaken from this as well. She calls the front desk.

"This is Dr. Fairchild in room 1212. I need maintenance to repair the rail on my deck. The room service attendant nearly fell to his death. The rail is loose. It is hanging from the veranda exterior wall by a rusty wire."

"I will put in a service request. I don't know how soon they will be there to fix it."

"I would think sooner than later. This is extremely dangerous. If you can't fix this by tomorrow, please move me to another room."

"Yes. I am not sure if we will be able to move you either. There are three doctor conventions; we are sold out."

"Unacceptable. Fix the rail. If not, get me a new room or a new hotel. Either way, the expense will be compensated by the Cote d'Azur Hotel."

It is a good thing I booked Dr. Kendall a room. Hopefully, I won't have to cancel or move either one of us to another hotel.

Dr. Fairchild brings the tray with her dinner back into the room. She removes the notebook from her briefcase and proceeds to read.

Chapter Fifty-Three

"Good morning. How is he doing?" the FBI agent on duty inquires.

"About the same, critical but stable," replies the nurse.

"Do you think he has a chance to pull through?"

"It is hard to say. I better go inside to check his vitals."

"Before you go, has he had any visitors?"

"No," replies the nurse.

"Is there anything that you can tell me?"

"All we know is that it is a miracle that he is alive. He was barely breathing when the medics arrived at his house."

"I understand he overdosed. The doctor said he thought it was suspicious, but wouldn't elaborate."

"He was taking nitroglycerin for his heart. It appears that he took too many. It actually caused a heart attack."

"The rumor in the hospital is that he is part of a murder investigation and that is why the FBI is involved," the nurse comments. "It's just idle talk."

"Put an end to the gossiping. We don't want his name on his chart. Your job and the others are at stake if you don't oblige," demands the FBI agent.

"So, your chitchat with me earlier was a test?" the nurse asks.

"Basically, yeah. The agents on their shifts have reported that there's talk within the hospital about John Doe. And I am here now to put an end to it, immediately."

The nurse continues to prop pillows under John Doe's head during her lecture from the FBI agent. Gently, she puts a warm, soft washcloth over his face, sprays shaving crème on his wrinkled cheeks, and slowly drags the razor from his cheekbone to his chin, leaving his skin silky and smooth to the touch.

"For the record, no one in the hospital ever intends to be malicious or careless. Mr. Doe's well-being is on everyone's priority list."

The nurse finishes shaving Mr. Doe. She squirts lotion into the palm of her hand. She rubs them together to warm the lotion before applying to Mr. Doe's arms and hands. Slowly, she rubs his forearm towards his hand. She notices that his finger twitched.

"Mr. Doe." She leans into his side, looking at his face, hoping his eyes will open to reveal their mystery color.

"Mr. Doe, please, if you can hear me, tap your finger," says the nurse.

There is no response by Mr. Doe. The nurse notes this event on his chart, adding an asterisk, emphasizing that all nurses should be watchful for any further movement.

"Mr. Doe will be coming around. I just feel it."

"Did I hear you talking to someone?" the FBI agent asks.

"You heard me talking to Mr. Doe. Part of working with coma patients is that we talk to them in hopes that they can hear us. Trust me, he won't spread any rumors."

"Are you trying to be cute?"

"No, just stating a fact." She walks down the corridor away from John Doe's room.

The agent pulls a chair from the nurses station and sits outside Mr. Doe's door.

Mr. Doe's finger twitches softly. He whispers, "Bailey, Bailey."

The agent thought he heard a voice coming from Mr. Doe's room. He walks to the nurses station.

"Excuse me, I think I heard the patient in room 2B speak."

"I don't think that is possible. He is a coma patient. It doesn't look very promising for him, meaning we don't think he will ever wake up."

"Enough Chatty Kathy. Please go to his room. I am telling you I heard a voice...something."

The floor nurse enters his room, checks his vitals, props his pillows, and fusses over him briefly.

"I am sorry, sir, there is no sign of anything," reports the nurse.

"Thanks for checking. I will go back to my post."

The nurse notes what the agent thought has transpired.

Chapter Fifty-Four

Dr. Fairchild has been sickened from what she has read in the inspector's notebook. He was the mystery Columbo that she labeled her shadow. He left cigar butts at the crime scenes she was working on. *How dare he scare the shit out of me.* The more she reads, the more infuriating she becomes. There are notes in detail about her attack, how he found her bound while standing, looking over her. Dr. Fairchild remembers that while passing out, she saw him at her feet.

"How could he have left me there without helping me?" she yelled outwardly.

She reads more of his notes where the inspector calls for help and explains how he has to pursue the assailant. His justification is he knows she would be okay. His notes regarding Libby's case is pretty intense, very thorough. The inspector's first suspect is Perry, but is then cleared.

This was why he had a fixation on me as a person of interest. I had the perfect motive. My fiancé was Libby's lover. Just when she has started to calm down, reading more about it brings back anger.

I have to pull myself together. I can't take this personally. What a nightmare!

What Dr. Fairchild is about to encounter from the inspector's notes turns her feelings from anger to respect.

From the inspector's notes.

At first, Dr. Fairchild was my main person of interest. I noticed that at each crime scene there was a person who appeared right after each killing, viewing as a spectator. I started to change my suspicions to that person and discovered that their intentions were to harm Dr. Fairchild. Until I am able to prove these suspicions, I will follow Dr. Fairchild as protection. I didn't want to be a nuisance to her cases. Brilliantly, I know she will solve and convict the killer or killers. I was keeping what I am doing a secret to protect her. I made arrangements with Dr. Fairchild to meet for dinner on August 16th. I want to tell her who I believe is the serial killer. She must know that she is in grave danger.

This was the inspector's last entry in his notebook.

We never made arrangements. I never talked to him. Who is the serial killer? Why did he lie and say we talked? Damn it, he didn't write who the serial killer is. "Who is it?!" she yells.

Dr. Fairchild frantically calls Korey; her heart was racing as though she just finished running a marathon in record time.

"Korey, please pickup," begs Dr. Fairchild.

No answer. It goes into his voicemail. She hangs up and puts the notebook in the black leather briefcase. The wind blows through the open balcony doors, the aroma of jasmine hovers into the room. The scent relaxes Dr. Fairchild momentarily. Her cell phone rings.

A little anxious, she answers, "Hello."

"Hey, beautiful, you called but didn't leave a message. What's going on?"

"I just finished reading the inspector's notebook. He knew who the serial killer is."

"Who is it? You sound hysterical."

"That's the problem. He didn't identify them in his notes."

"You are kidding me, right?"

"I wish I was. I am serious. The inspector indicated that he made a dinner engagement with me to discuss his suspicions. He was planning to disclose the killer or killers the night he was murdered."

"When did he contact you?"

"He never did. I don't know who he thought he was talking to, but it wasn't me. Korey, I feel like I am losing my mind. People see me in places that I've never been to or had discussions with me that never took place."

"Did he give any clue of who it might be?"

"No. He had been following me to protect me. He said I started off as being a person of interest, but then he noticed I was being stalked. He was genuinely concerned for my safety. His notes confirmed there is a serial killer, possibly two working together, and that I am the target."

"What the hell?"

"That's how he started off, believing that there were two killers. But then he confirmed one killer, and she is a woman."

"You are sounding a little relaxed."

"Talking to you always brings me back to reality into a calmer state of mind. Were you and Dr. Kendall successful with figuring out Paddy's clues?"

"Not much success. Still points to accidental. I am sorry. We believe it was murder, but we are having a hard time proving it."

"I know in my heart it wasn't an overdose."

"The clues don't make any sense, a riddle that runs in circles. Dr. Kendall confirmed there were traces of a sleeping drug, doxylamine, in his bloodstream. It's a common drug that can be purchased over the counter. It is pretty potent when given in large dosage."

Except for the sigh she mustered from feeling defeated, Dr. Fairchild is silent.

"Are you there?" Korey asks.

"I am here, just a little discouraged. I feel like I have let him down."

"Listen, Dr. Kendall said that she will spend more time and will reanalyze the test."

"How long do you plan on staying in New Jersey?"

"I thought we decided we would arrive this weekend. Are you having second thoughts?"

"No. My mind is a little forgetful these days. I finished earlier than I had anticipated. Would you be able to fly in sooner?"

"I could see what is available tomorrow."

"Would you like to spend some time with me looking for a gallery?"

"So, you are going to go for it? I would love to go. We need a little distraction, some fun. I don't think Dr. Kendall can come before the weekend."

"That's fine. I am doing this for Paddy, in honor of him. He was always my inspiration."

"Who knows, maybe Dr. Fairchild will resurrect an old passion?" Korey states.

"I haven't painted in years. I look forward to running a gallery and retiring from the years of Corpse Unlimited."

"That's a ghastly way of describing your career. Do you have a place in mind for your new venture?"

"I do. There's an old office building in Montreal that has been vacant for a couple of years. It needs some work. But with a little elbow grease, we could have it ready for a showing in a couple of months."

"We, meaning you and me?" Korey asks.

"Sure, it'll be a lot of fun. Can you imagine the thrill of choosing paintings, designing the gallery, and finding statues that correlate with certain paintings and a theme that we change periodically?"

Dr. Fairchild is ecstatic. She sounds like a schoolgirl describing her dress for a prom.

"It sounds like a lot of work and expensive."

"It's the kind of work that I want to embrace, a great distraction that we both can use. And the expense, it's worth every penny."

"It is nice to hear you enthused about something. You went from fear and discouragement to joy and full of life. This is definitely the rebirth of a passion that died."

"Trust me, I am not going to walk away from these cases and leave them unsolved. It still reigns as a high priority. The gallery is a commitment that I will fulfill in honor of Paddy."

"Reflections," Dr. Fairchild blurts out.

"What are you talking about? Reflections of what?"

"That will be the name of the gallery."

"That didn't take long," responds Korey.

"One of my first portraits was of my grandmother. It was Paddy's favorite. I named the painting 'Reflections.'"

"The portrait is my grandmother looking into a mirror. The reflection is me as a child. It is beautiful, a grown woman looking into a mirror and her reflection is a child. Paddy always said how much I looked like my grandmother. Paddy said he was amazed at how I captured her resemblance so perfectly to the little girl."

"Oh, my God, Korey, that is Paddy's clue."

"You are losing me."

"Remember, twice, his clues indicated reflection from a mirror. That's it. Once we figured out whose reflection was in the mirror, we will know his killer. It wasn't accidental."

"You are determined, or you will not accept the fact it was an accident. No, it is not a fact. Where is the proof to state otherwise?"

"Korey, is Dr. Kendall still there?"

"Yes. She is in the autopsy room?"

"Please have her call me right away."

"Yes, ma'am."

"Don't be a smart ass, and thank you."

Korey shakes his head in disbelief over his conversation with Dr. Fairchild. He walks down the corridor of the morgue, realizes where he is at, and picks up his pace. He then sprints into the autopsy room.

"Dr. Kendall, sorry for barging in. Bailey still believes Paddy's death wasn't accidental. She has a theory she wants to discuss with you. Call her as soon as possible."

"She's not budging?"

"Nope, she is like a dog on a bone; a forensic anthropologist on corpse's bones. I don't think there's much of a difference."

"Maybe that is why she has earned the reputation of being the best forensic anthropologist across two countries."

"You are right. She is the best. I think it's the stubborn Irish in her." Korey cackles.

"I will call her soon. I am almost done with the report on this doctor who died from a heart attack during sex; too much Viagra."

"Well, at least, he was having fun. Did you know Bailey was an artist?"

"Really? I didn't know."

"Her paintings are exquisite. She has a real talent...beautiful work. I am amazed how she captures the expression on people; the paintings radiate the smallest detail. They are impressive. She's planning to retire and open a gallery in Montreal."

"I didn't know that about her. It shouldn't be a surprise. She is a woman with many talents."

"We know how Bailey comes across—very serious, business-only type, straight to the point, and a little dry," says Korey.

"Where are you going with this?" Dr. Kendall asks.

"When I was talking to her, she went from being sad, confused, and scared when we were discussing the cases. But as soon as she mentioned opening a gallery, a whole new Bailey emerged. It was a pleasure to hear enthusiasm from her. I believe opening a gallery would ease her transition into retirement."

"I don't see Dr. Fairchild ever retiring from forensics. These cases are personal. They have hit her hard. I am telling you she will retire from the heartaches from the cases, but not from forensics. Forensics is what pumps her blood through her veins. The gallery is her passion. She will have the best of both worlds.

"A gallery where?" Dr. Kendall asks.

"In downtown Montreal. She already has the location and name."

"Really? Don't hold back now, tell me the name."

"Reflections."

"I like it."

"When she told me the name of the gallery, that's what trumped her to believe Paddy's death isn't accidental, that he was murdered."

"All of that from a name of a gallery?" Dr. Kendall asks.

"It's not just any name. It is Reflections. She will go more into the details when you call."

"Well, now my curiosity is piqued."

"What she said is incredible. It makes sense. We just have to prove it."

"I have some vacation time, and I desperately need to get away. I was planning to take some time off. I understand Canada is a beautiful place to visit this time of year."

"Bailey would love to have you there."

"Did she say when she wants to open the gallery?" Dr. Kendall asks.

"In our conversation, she stated within a few months. This could be a lot of fun as Bailey professes."

"Bailey is adamant about not having any unsolved cases. She's on a roll and not giving up."

"Good, neither are we."

"When are you going back to Canada?" Dr. Kendall asks.

"I am leaving tomorrow morning," he replies.

"I'll let Bailey know that I will leave in a couple of days. Korey, would you please book me a room at Bailey's hotel?" Dr. Kendall requests.

"No problem. I will when I get to my hotel. Have a safe trip. I will see you soon," says Korey.

"Korey, wait. Here, take these notes that I have documented on Mr. Fairchild. There's a hunch that I am working on. If I am right, it could affect Bailey."

"What do you mean affect Bailey?"

"I really shouldn't say anything until I have concrete evidence. There is a snag that I need to get untangled."

"What's the snag, if I may ask?"

"Getting the approval to have another lab do the testing on Dr. Fairchild's DNA and fingerprints. Something anomalous came up from Mr. Fairchild's evidence: another set of fingerprints at the crime scene. I am not an expert in blood tests, only the bones. I do some analysis. I don't have the high tech equipment that is needed for what I am looking for. As soon as I get the approval, I will have DC rush on the analysis."

"It will take weeks."

"I have an old friend who owes me a few favors. He is the chief medical examiner for DC."

"DC sounds serious."

"If my hunch is correct, it is serious. Sorry that I've detained you. Please don't say anything to Dr. Fairchild until I have facts."

"I won't say a word. I am glad you shared with me."

Korey leaves the lab. His skin grows clammy. Her lack of eye contact raised suspicion about the lab analysis. *What did Dr. Kendall discover? She has hard facts. She knows more than what she is admitting to. What is serious enough to cause her to lie and avoid telling me the truth?* Korey thought.

Dr. Kendall locks up the lab cabinet and adds an entry to her journal: CASE CLOSED; noting the cause of death as an overdose of Viagra.

This was an easy one. I should have told Korey the truth. Guilt riddles through her. Fear struggles with her guilt. One threat was all she needed to keep this a secret. *I was wrong for not showing the threatening letter to Korey. The words 'I am in mortal danger' was enough for me.* Mortal danger haunts Dr. Kendall's mind.

Dr. Kendall isn't focused on the dark cold corridor that leads her to the stairwell. The fear and guilt harbor in her soul. They have her course of direction in autopilot. A person grabs Dr. Kendall from behind. He pulls her close to his body, simultaneously covering her mouth. Her body stiffens in apprehension. Instantly, she is jolted from a state of autopilot to reality.

"Shhh, it's Perry."

A sharp pain penetrates his hand before he can explain his stalking behavior.

"Damn it, I am bleeding," shrieks Perry.

"What the hell are you doing, sneaking up behind me, grabbing me like some psycho stalker?" Dr. Kendall blurts out a guttural scream.

He grabs her arm.

"Please, quietly come out from the corridor, step in here," Perry points towards his direction.

"This better be good. You scared the shit out of me," yelled Dr. Kendall, her voice struggles to control quavering.

"You are being stalked. They are down the other stairwell. As I was coming to your lab, they were standing outside the lab door listening in. When Korey left, they started to follow him. They saw me...we gazed at each other, and we walked down separate corridors."

"Did you see who it was?"

"The lights are out in both corridors. All I saw was a silhouette. What I do know? It was a woman or a man wearing a big floppy hat," Perry states.

"I think she is the same person I saw at the airport when I was waiting for Bailey. This woman was at the baggage carousel, wearing a big floppy hat. They have striking characteristics."

"Why are you here? It's not like we are friends."

"You can hate me all you want. We both have one common dominator and that is Bailey's well-being and safety."

"You have a strange way of expressing how you feel. Where should I start? Breaking her heart, almost getting her killed, lies and deceit. Should I carry on?"

"You've made your point. Believe it or not I want to make it up to her. She is fed up and doesn't want to see me. It's understandable."

"Do you blame her?"

"No, that is why I need you. As a district attorney I do have some pull and power. Have you been contacted by the FBI?"

"Why are you asking?"

"You seem preoccupied, a little scared."

"Gees, I wonder why. Yes, they are taking over the investigation of the cases that involved Bailey. They are more focused on Paddy's case. I was surprised that it wasn't Libby's."

"What are they asking from you? Or, I will rephrase the question, what are they demanding you do?"

"They want Paddy's DNA and fingerprint analysis to go to DC."

"Don't send them."

"Mr. Sinclair, I took their demand more as a threat than an order. Convince me why I should listen or believe you."

"That's fair. First, you must promise me that you will not repeat what I tell you to anyone, especially Bailey. What I am going to disclose is critical for Bailey and Paddy's safety and life."

"Mr. Fairchild is dead."

"No, he isn't. That is what I need to tell you. Can we talk?"

"I have a condo on the shores of Atlantic City. You can't miss it. It is the second condo from the marina. You won't need an address. In one hour."

Still shaken from her stalking ordeal, Dr. Kendall embraces the thought of an apple martini on the terrace, listening to the white cap waves crashing against the rocks. A beautiful afternoon for a cocktail are her thoughts, a visual that taunts her mind. Slowly, she drags her hand across her mouth, wiping the saliva away. The drive along the shores of Atlantic City is relaxing. The convertible top is down, inviting the ocean breeze displaying a whirlwind that whistles through her hair. The sultry hot sun warms her fair skin. Dr. Kendall is doing everything she can to avoid her ordeal with Perry.

Chapter Fifty-Five

"Delicious. This should do it. Nicely sweet, slightly bitter, and smooth, a perfect apple martini," mumbles Dr. Kendall.

The first sip was a sensual event, an explosion for every taste bud.

An incredible sight for sore eyes, she thought as Perry struts across the sand towards her condo. *Too bad he can be such a jerk. He is delightful. I understand the addiction Dr. Fairchild has towards him. He is intoxicating.* Her thoughts are embedded on Perry.

"Hi, I see you found the place," Dr. Kendall leans over the terrace and motions Perry towards the side of the condo.

"Come around to the front. The door is open."

Perry walks through an enchanted garden of colorful flowers. Mist from a waterfall sprays on him as he enters the condo. The walls are made of imported glass from Italy, each etched with a different flower design. A baby grand piano greets Perry as he walks towards the terrace.

Perry is enamored with the Italian marble floor that carves a pathway to the terrace. On each side of the six-foot long corridor are tropical flowers refreshed by the air mist that rest upon each branch and the flower petals, enhancing their color. The greenery and the array of bright colors cast from the flowers have a natural calming affect. A brilliant way to welcome a guest.

"What a setup. This is beautiful."

"I just made an apple martini. Would you like one?"

"Yes, please."

"With or without ice?"

"On the rocks."

"I read the reports on Mr. Fairchild. There is no way that he can be alive. It would have to be a miracle," says Dr. Kendall, her voice cold as death.

"That is exactly what it is, a miracle. The paramedics stated that Mr. Fairchild was barely alive. Their tenacious attempts saved him. In the police report, it is documented that Mr. Fairchild threw up."

"His doctor explained that when he threw up, it emptied his stomach of nitroglycerin. And the time of when he purged; saved his life."

"The doctor is correct."

"Where is Mr. Fairchild? How is he doing?" Dr. Kendall asks.

"In the hospital. He is alive, but not doing well. He is listed as critical. Paddy is in a coma."

"You refer to Mr. Fairchild as Paddy. Did you know him personally?"

"I did. He didn't like being called Mr. Fairchild. That's Paddy, very down to earth."

"I would think telling Bailey about Paddy would help him."

"I said the same thing to the FBI. They don't want Bailey to know. Their theory is if she knows, it could jeopardize their hunt for the killer and put both of them in danger. Basically, they are using Bailey as bait."

"Perry, this is very hard for me. I have become close to Bailey. I respect her as a colleague and a friend. She is so heartbroken over the loss of Paddy. To me it's criminal."

Perry can see that. Dr. Kendall's eyes are haunted by an inner anxiety.

"I am struggling with those same feelings since the FBI approached me a few days ago."

"How did the FBI know where to contact you?"

"That's the confusing part. They did a thorough investigation of everyone who attended Paddy's services. The FBI stated that they received an anonymous call saying I was there. Part of their investigation was to talk to all attendees at the service. Because Bailey and I are not talking, out of respect for her, I purposely didn't sign the guest book, I didn't mingled with anyone, and I stayed a mystery. Or so I thought."

"I was there. I didn't see you."

"That is what makes this so confusing. I was in the balcony by myself. I made sure no one saw me.

"Bailey hates me. She told me to stay away from her. I didn't want to upset her. She had been through enough turmoil. I do care about her."

"Are we able to see Paddy?"

"No. He is heavily sedated. There are FBI agents guarding him around the clock."

"Wow, this is serious."

"If Paddy pulls through, they will be on him like a duck on a June bug."

"The poor guy will probably wish he didn't wake up."

"There is something else to consider. Paddy could have amnesia."

"Would you like a refill?" Dr. Kendall asks.

"That would be great."

"I am planning to leave for Canada tomorrow. Korey said Bailey needs to see me immediately."

"What time is your flight?"

"I am leaving tomorrow afternoon. And when will you go back to Canada?"

"Tomorrow morning," replies Perry. "Well, it would have been more enjoyable to have shared the same flight back to Canada with you."

"Let's not go there Don Juan. Cool your jets."

"I only meant as friends sharing a flight together," he replies with a sheepish smile.

"Sure, I don't buy it. Let's keep it strictly business, for Bailey's sake," states Dr. Kendall.

Perry tries to keep the dialogue going between them. He enjoys Dr. Kendall's company and her beauty.

Dr. Kendall affects me differently more than any other woman. I would like to get to know her...more than just professional. Maybe not a good idea as Dr. Kendall insisted, but that's part of her charm— playing hard to get, he begins to think.

"Did you know that Bailey is opening a gallery in Montreal? Korey mentioned the gallery to me this morning."

"I dated her for years and didn't know she was an artist. It makes sense why she has a love for art."

"That is why I am leaving for Montreal. Korey has been shipping her art pieces from Paddy's gallery on Dauphin Island to a warehouse in Canada."

"Hard to believe, but I guess she really is planning to retire."

"I'll bet odds that she won't retire. I have worked with her. She was my professor. And she is too devoted to forensics. Forensics has a mystical hold on her.

"The three of us are meeting to go over the cases. Bailey wants to push hard to find concrete evidence to convict the serial killer."

"I know how she is. I worked with her on a case years ago. It took years to solve. Other forensic anthropologists quit; they were letting it get cold. Bailey took it over. She spent seven years learning, breathing, and thinking like the serial killer."

"Was the killer convicted?"

"No, killed being apprehended."

"Bailey will not quit no matter how difficult or dangerous the case may be. You'll leave tomorrow for Canada?"

"I was, but I've decided to visit Paddy instead. I want to be there when he wakes up. It is the least I can do for Bailey."

"I won't send the DNA and fingerprint analysis to DC. I will stall."

"That will be great. I am not sure who to trust in the FBI. I am still curious why Paddy's death outweighed Libby's and the inspector's murders."

"I agree. It is not logical. Hopefully, we will be able to make some sense of it soon. Call me as soon as anything changes with Paddy," Dr. Kendall requests.

"I will. I had a lovely time. I am going to leave so I can get a flight to Alabama tonight."

"Before you go, who do you think was in the corridor at my lab?"

"Honestly, I'm not sure. Their silhouette was either of a small man impersonating a woman or it was a woman. Make sure you call me when you leave and when you arrive in Canada."

"Thank you, Perry."

Perry leaves Dr. Kendall's condo. The quietness that normally has been Dr. Kendall's tranquility is now unsettling her nerves. Staying alone is not happening. Dr. Kendall picks up her Blackberry.

"Good afternoon, this is the Radcliffe Inn. How may I help you?" the reservation clerk asks.

"Do you have a room available for this evening?"

"Please hold while I check."

Holding seems like an eternity. The apple martini no longer calms her down. Instead, it is making her nauseous. Her conversation with Perry leaves her panicky. The Radcliffe Inn is next to the airport.

"Hello, we do have a room."

"Great. I would like to check in this evening. I will see you soon. Thank you."

Dr. Kendall packs and is out of her condo within two hours.

Chapter Fifty-Six

"Well, Korey, what do you think? With a little work and some paint, we can have this place looking like a gallery."

"It has potential. I guess it takes an artist's eye."

"A little color, proper lighting, and the paintings it will be fantastic," Dr. Fairchild states with glee.

"When do you plan to open?"

"The grand opening will be in three weeks."

"Isn't that cutting it pretty close? There is a lot to do. We need manpower."

"I have already hired a crew, and they will start in an hour."

"So, it didn't matter what I thought about this place. Your mind was already set."

"Pretty much!" She giggles coyly.

"What is on the agenda for me?" Korey asks.

"How about coordinating with the electricians or marketing programs. I already have a floor plan that I designed. Here is a copy. I have been meeting with an architect. I will need someone to supervise where the lights are to be installed. It's important that the lights are positioned to enhance the paintings. I have highlighted those positions in yellow."

"Grass never grows under your feet."

Dr. Fairchild smiles flirtatiously at Korey.

"When will Dr. Kendall arrive?"

"She will arrive at two o'clock today. I will pick her up. We already made the hotel arrangements. Dr. Kendall is staying where you are."

"That's perfect. We will spend some time reviewing the cases. Then I would like to show her the gallery."

"This is the happiest and giddiest I have ever seen you behave."

"I feel alive; a chance for a new beginning, a memorial for Paddy. I miss him so much. This is what he would have wanted. Korey, come with me."

Dr. Fairchild hurdles Korey to the center of the foyer.

"Right here is where I want to hang the Mona Lisa."

She points to a wide marble pillar standing directly in the middle of the foyer. This is the only attractive structure existing in the building.

"The electricians are here. Please work with them on the lights. I am going to start an invitation list."

"How many are you inviting?"

"Two hundred," says Dr. Fairchild. "When the gallery is completed, there won't be another gallery in Canada like Reflections. Everything will be state-of-the-art."

"I am proud of you. You are truly taking this new mission in your life to its fullest."

"Who is the gentleman walking with his hands behind his back? An inquisitive looking chap. Do you know him?" Korey asks.

"No. Would you be a dear and see what he wants? Thanks, I will be in the back."

Korey approaches the gentleman with confidence.

"May I help you?"

"I am looking for Dr. Fairchild."

"And you are?" Korey asks.

"Dr. Alan Miller. She doesn't know me directly."

"Then how does she know you indirectly?"

"From many years ago. She knows my son."

The mystery has stirred Korey's protective side and has gotten him aggressive in his tone. He grabs the man's arm and starts heading him towards the door.

"Sir, please, I don't mean any harm to Dr. Fairchild. It is a business opportunity for the gallery."

Their voices echoes throughout the gallery. The mystery has sparked her curiosity. She approaches them.

"Excuse me, I am Dr. Fairchild. How may I help you?"

"I am Dr. Alan Miller from Santa Barbara."

"You are a long way from home. Are you in forensics?"

"No, nothing that important. I am an oral surgeon."

"That's important, maybe not as dangerous."

"Unless you count the times when patients threaten to kill you if you hurt them, or an occasional bite on the hand," says Dr. Miller.

Dr. Fairchild likes Dr. Miller's humor and is impressed with his Armani attire. It is apparent that he aged gracefully. His distinguished salt and pepper hair accentuates his handsome face.

"I think you may have me beaten according to our occupations."

"Do you remember my son, Abraham? His mother was Alayna Dupree."

"I do remember Baby Abe. You were the couple who adopted Abe. Is your wife here?"

"No. She couldn't make it. We have a practice together. She is holding down the fort."

"Is she a dental hygienist?"

"No. She's an oral surgeon."

"I didn't mean to be offensive," Dr. Fairchild apologizes.

"No worries, no offense taken."

"Abraham is our only child. He is a wonderful young man. Just finished his studies at Ecole des Beaux-Arts in France. He loves living in France. He was valedictorian. Abraham study two years at the American University of Paris before going on to Ecole des Beaux-Arts. He has been painting since he was twelve, a natural gift."

"Does Abraham have a preference of art?"

"He paints many different styles. His eye for watercolors is breathtaking. Abraham has quite a collection of his art work."

"How can I help?" Dr. Fairchild asks.

"Would it be possible for Abraham to display some of his paintings in your gallery? He is young, but mature beyond his years. I don't think you will be disappointed."

"When could I meet Abraham?"

"Now, if you would like to. He is over here, mixed in with the workers and the abstract artwork."

As soon as Abraham turned to face them, Dr. Fairchild knew instantly that Abe is Alayna's son. He is as handsome as she was beautiful. His dark silky hair as a baby is now blond and as radiant as his mother's. Abe's big, almond-shaped eyes are outlined by thick black lashes that magnify the gray-blue color, almost a perfect match to Alayna. The closer Abe approached, the more handsome he became.

"Abraham, please come here. This is Dr. Fairchild."

"How do you do, ma'am?" Abraham extends his right hand towards Dr. Fairchild for a subtle warm handshake. "A pleasure to meet you," says Abraham.

"The pleasure is mine. Please call me Bailey. Ma'am makes me sound old."

"You are not old, but I must call you Dr. Fairchild out of respect."

"Okay."

What a gentleman. His handshake was friendly and was delivered with a sense of confidence, she thinks.

"Your father has proudly told us of your accomplishments as a talented artist. I am interested in seeing your artwork."

"Thank you," Abraham boasts.

"How soon can you bring them here?"

"We have them with us," replies Dr. Miller.

"That's fantastic. Bring them to the gallery tonight at seven o'clock. Do you have any experience working in a gallery?"

"I worked at the Francois de Laux Gallery while going to art school. I was the gallery manager."

"There are deadlines that I have to meet by the end of the month. The grand opening is scheduled in one month. Do you live in Santa Barbara? May I ask why you are in Canada?"

"We have family living in Montreal. They told us about the new gallery opening. I plan to relocate. I will be staying with my aunt and uncle. When do you want me to start?"

"How about tomorrow, 9:00 a.m. sharp?"

Dr. Miller and Abraham shook Dr. Fairchild's hand, thanking her for this opportunity.

"I will see you tonight at seven."

"A charming and bright young man. He is absolutely nothing like his mother."

"I was impressed with Abraham and his father. You can tell he is well loved. How do you know his mother?" asks Korey.

"His mother wasn't fortunate to have love in her life; it was the opposite for him. There was a serial killer that took seven years to be captured. It was his mother. Her childhood was abusive. She was raped by her stepfather and stepbrother. Alayna was fourteen when she had Abe.

"It is evident that Abraham's family adores and genuinely loves him."

"Did you get to know his mother?"

"There was one occasion, prior to her capture, when I met with Alayna. I tried talking her into turning herself in. That lifestyle was all she knew. She was a beautiful lost soul. It was hopeless and sad.

"I need a favor. Please run a background check on Abraham."

"Do you think there's a problem?"

"It won't hurt to be sure. I am not taking any risk."

"Oh, look at the time. I have to pick Dr. Kendall up," says Korey.

"I forgot she was coming with all the excitement," says Dr. Fairchild.

"Please suggest dinner for the three of us after I meet with Abraham."

"What time for dinner reservations?"

"Is eight okay? I can't imagine being longer than an hour. Pick me up then."

Chapter Fifty-Seven

"You're right on time. Please come in. Dr. Miller and Abraham, it is a pleasure to see you again."

"Good evening, Dr. Fairchild. We brought four paintings. My other pieces are in Santa Barbara. We can have them shipped in time for the grand opening," says Abraham.

"These are beautiful. This piece is stunning."

Dr. Fairchild points to an artwork that is propped against the marble pillar.

"I have your first assignment for tomorrow. I want this abstract to hang on the opposite side of the Mona Lisa.

"I noticed 'Mosaic' is written on the back on the painting. Is this the name of the abstract painting?"

"Yes, Dr. Fairchild."

"Impressive and stunning paintings. I would like to display all your artwork. You portray a superb blend of the pastels. You have an amazing talent for encapsulating every detail. I will need you to start tomorrow morning. An important task that I would like you to do, before working with the electricians, is order nameplates for all of your art." Dr. Fairchild smiles with admiration.

"Thank you, Dr. Fairchild."

Abraham shakes Dr. Fairchild's hand with the same warm, friendly hold, except that this time, it is with more confidence.

The meeting with Abraham is less than an hour. Dr. Fairchild looks at her watch. *I still have some time before Korey picks me up.*

Dr. Fairchild moves the art pieces to the locations where she wants them displayed. She stares adoringly at the 'Mosaic,' proud of Abraham. Dr. Fairchild moves closer to the painting, studying the abstract lines that flow in perfect unison. Then the back door suddenly slams, breaking her concentration.

"Hello, may I help you?"

Startled, Dr. Fairchild's voice barely carries out a sound.

"Dr. Miller, Abraham?" Dr. Fairchild calls out their names while she quietly walks to the back of the gallery.

"Did you forget something?"

There are footsteps approaching behind Dr. Fairchild. She pivots her body to the left, but fate intercedes. A heavy object grazes her temple, embedding a sharp pain to her head. She drops to the floor. The intruder stands over Dr. Fairchild and stares coldly at her limp body. Their mission is interrupted by the pounding on the front door.

"Bailey, it's Korey. I am with Dr. Kendall."

Korey pounds again on the door, a little more aggressive. He tries to open the door; it's locked.

"Bailey!" he calls.

Dr. Kendall peeks in the window. She sees a body lying on the floor.

"Korey, look, there is someone on the floor. I can't tell if it's Bailey."

"I am going to the back entrance. Stay here."

Dr. Kendall sees Korey entering into the gallery. He kneels down to the limp body.

"Bailey, come on, wake up."

She moves. Dazed, she rubs the side of her head. There is a warm sticky substance on her fingers.

"You are bleeding. I don't think you need stitches. What happened?" Korey asks.

"I am not sure. I heard footsteps behind me. I turned and that's all I remember."

"Did you see anyone?"

"No!"

Korey holds Dr. Fairchild's arm. He helps her stand up. They slowly walk to the front door. He opens the door for Dr. Kendall.

"What happened?" Dr. Kendall asks.

"I was closing up after Abraham and his father left."

"We should have run a background check on Abraham before we committed to any business," Korey snaps.

"There isn't anything wrong with Abraham."

"How can you be so sure? After they left, this happens," Korey snaps.

"How do you feel?" asks Dr. Kendall.

"I am okay. I have a headache."

"We need to clean you up. I think we should skip dinner. We can meet tomorrow," says Dr. Kendall.

"No. We are still going to dinner. I don't need any stitches. I will freshen up, and we will go as planned.

"Before we leave, I would like to see if anything is missing."

"The back door was wide open. I didn't see anyone," says Korey.

"Dr. Fairchild, are you sure dinner is okay?" asks Dr. Kendall compassionately.

"Yes, absolutely." Dr. Fairchild replies.

"Don't argue with her. She is stubborn and you won't win," says Korey.

"Come over here. Look at his artwork. They are fabulous."

"Unbelievable! Abraham did these?"

"Yes. I am telling you he is talented and a well-educated young man. It wasn't Abraham who attacked me. He has too much to lose.

"Well, I am ready to go. Everything seems to be here. Please help me lock up. I am starving."

Korey is locking up the back part of the gallery when he notices a gasoline can behind the garbage can next to the doorway.

"Bailey, would you please come here?"

"What's going on?"

"Look by the garbage can. Would there be any reason why you would need gas?"

"No, unless one of the workers put it there. Tomorrow, I will ask the crew not to leave any flammables in or around the gallery.

"Or, do you think I may have stopped the intruder, a possible arsonist? They probably didn't expect anyone to be here."

"If that's true, you are the target, Bailey."

"Let's go to dinner. I have set the alarm."

Dr. Fairchild isn't as hungry as she thinks. The Cobb salad wasn't satisfying, but the glass of cabernet eased the headache that was pounding to an annoying pulse.

"Maybe we should call it a night. We have sat here for over an hour, hardly ate our food, and haven't spoken a full sentence between the three of us," says Dr. Fairchild.

"It's late and we are tired. After a good night's rest, we can meet tomorrow morning. We need to work on the cases."

"May we have our check please?" Korey asks the waitress. Korey then says to his companions, "Are you, ladies, ready to go? Your chariot awaits you."

"You always say the right thing at the right time." Dr. Fairchild winks at Korey.

"Thanks for dinner."

Korey opens the car door for Dr. Fairchild and Dr. Kendall.

"Dr. Fairchild, I have to check in. I'll meet you in the lobby," says Dr. Kendall. "I am exhausted. It was a long flight. Glad you are okay. I enjoyed spending some time with you."

"I missed you, too," Korey says to Dr. Kendall.

"You are opening a gallery. I am proud of you. You are definitely not boring," says Dr. Kendall.

"Thank you, but some men I have dated would probably state otherwise," says Dr. Fairchild.

"Funny. What does that mean?" asks Dr. Kendall.

"Never mind. I am just being silly, a side effect from the bump on my head."

"Do you need me to pick you up in the morning?" asks Korey.

"Yes. Thanks for the door service. Sleep well," answers Dr. Kendall.

Dr. Fairchild and Dr. Kendall leave the car to check in.

"Good evening," says Dr. Fairchild to the hotel door man as they walk past, entering the lobby of the hotel.

"Good evening, ladies. May I have your luggage delivered to your room?" he asks.

"No, thank you," replies Dr. Kendall.

"May we have the key for Dr. Kendall?"

"I already have it. While you were talking to Korey, I took care of it. I will thank Korey tomorrow."

"Bailey, I have to ask. What did you mean when you said that the men you've dated would find you boring? You kind of implied that you've dated Korey."

"We didn't exactly date. We had a passionate moment where lust took over. Korey thought there was more. I...I value us being great friends. We work well together. I don't want to jeopardize any of that. I will be the first to admit that when it comes to men, I suck. I excel in my career with no problems."

"I think you are being too hard on yourself. You are a brilliant forensic criminologist. I haven't known or worked with anyone that is as thorough or diligent in this field as you. And for your love life, maybe you just haven't met the right one. Relationships are hard. Society has produced dysfunctional people. Dysfunction is now the normal. He is out there, sometimes right under our noses. Tell me if I am wrong, but you thrive off challenges. It's who you are," says Dr. Kendall.

"You are correct. Most of the men that I have dated are not challenging and are boring."

"How was dating District Attorney Perry Sinclair? You dated him for some time."

"We dated for about five years. It was challenging, but for all the wrong reasons. The relationship was an emotional nightmare."

"I find Korey to be anything but boring. He is intelligent and not bad to look at either," Dr. Kendall comments.

"I agree. I just don't have the quality of time that is required for a healthy relationship. I know I am not the easiest person to deal with. I am telling you, I suck at this."

Chapter Fifty-Eight

Dr. Kendall tosses and turns throughout the night. She is unable to fall asleep. Her thoughts race over and over again, dissecting the evidence and clues from the cases. *The DNA matches the same DNA at Libby's crime scene and the inspector's; its Bailey's DNA. The killer is thorough and meticulous, doesn't leave any fingerprints. This could only be done by someone as brilliant as Bailey. She has the motive for both killings. No, I refuse to believe it could be Bailey.* She toils with these thoughts that Bailey could be guilty. *These are horrible thoughts.*

Dr. Kendall's intuition isn't kicking in, and this scares her, to think that she is thinking the worst of Bailey. She surrenders to sleeplessness and decides to get up. Dr. Kendall spreads her notes across the bed. She rereads them word for word.

"Damn it. Why can't I find the answer? What am I missing?" Dr. Kendall yells.

There is a pounding coming from the connecting door where Dr. Fairchild is staying.

"Katherine, are you okay? shouts Dr. Fairchild.

"Yes, I am okay. I was going over my notes and got into my work. You haven't called me Katherine since the shoot up in your lab."

"Would you like a glass of wine? I was pouring one at the time of your one-sided conversation." Dr. Fairchild laughs.

"That would be nice," Dr. Kendall opens the connecting door to greet Dr. Fairchild.

"A toast to you," says Dr. Fairchild.

"I apologize if I disturbed you."

Dr. Kendall inhales the aroma lingering from the glass, enjoying the bittersweet fragrance. The flavor is as enchanting as the fragrance.

"Thanks, this is what I needed."

"You didn't disturb me. I was having a hard time dropping off. My mind keeps racing over the cases. There has to be a common dominator between the cases."

"That's why I wasn't sleeping either," says Dr. Kendall.

"I can see by the mess on your bed. Any thoughts?" Dr. Fairchild asks.

"Only that the evidence is pointing to you. It's your DNA, and you have motive for both killings."

"Thanks for your candor."

"I am not implying anything, just stating the facts," replies Dr. Kendall.

"The only fingerprints are yours. I understand Libby was murdered in your car and conveniently in a car wash to rid of any other evidence. At Paddy's crime scene, you could have DNA and fingerprints there as well, but you were never around the inspector. This is the only piece to the puzzle that doesn't fit."

"That's where I am stumped, too. The only explanation I came up with was I am being framed. Someone mysteriously was able to get my DNA for the setup. Well, I have a bottle of wine that I don't want to drink by myself. There are notes to go over and neither one of us can sleep. Care to join me?"

Dr. Fairchild holds up the bottle of wine, smiles an invitation she hopes Dr. Kendall will accept.

"Hell, I am game. Let's review this stack. It's Paddy's medical examiner analysis and the police report. You might be interested in Korey's theory about the clues that Paddy left. Korey had fixation on the coat rack. Seems Paddy's initials were reversed, which then read 'FP.' Korey felt the 'FP' represented the fireplace. He said your picture is facing the mirror above the fireplace, same as your picture on the nightstand facing a mirror on the dresser. Interestingly, Korey concluded that the mirrors possibly indicate a reflection."

"A reflection of what? Ironically, that is the name of the gallery," says Dr. Fairchild.

"That's where we both came to a dead end," says Dr. Kendall.

"Another clue is the teacup, meaning a woman. There was a porcelain shoe found on the mantle. We are not sure if that was a clue from Paddy or is always placed there."

"I didn't know a porcelain shoe was found on the mantle."

"Why are you so concerned over the shoe? What's the significance?" Dr. Kendall asks.

"My grandmother collected Victorian porcelain shoes. She displayed them across the window sill. They would never be any place else."

"What does it mean?" inquired Dr. Kendall.

"A reflection of a woman. Possibly, someone my grandmother knew."

"Do you have any idea who this might be?

"None at this moment. I was a little girl when my grandmother died. I don't remember any woman, and Paddy never talked about anyone."

"How does this connect with Libby's death?" Dr. Kendall asks.

"That's a good question. I don't know," replies Dr. Fairchild.

"Tomorrow, I will talk to Mr. Wade. He is Paddy's attorney. Maybe he knows of someone from the past."

"You mean later today. It's one o'clock in the morning."

"We've been at this for three hours. I feel we have made some progress. I am going to bed. I will be starting my day in a few hours," says Dr. Fairchild.

"Thanks for the wine and your company. We will figure this out. Good night," Dr. Kendall assures.

"Good night. I had a good time, too."

Dr. Fairchild coils into the goose down comforter. "Paddy, if you can hear me, please guide me. This is so hard. Maybe I am too close." These were Dr. Fairchild's last softly spoken words before she fell into a slumber.

Dr. Kendall's body is vacuumed by the goose down comforter. She nestles her head onto the oversized pillow. She taps the base of the lamp, welcoming the darkness. A light peers beneath the door, exposing a shadow of an image pacing slowly back and forth.

"Hello, hello!" Her voice degenerates to a childish whimper.

No response. Dr. Kendall checks the safety latch on the door to confirm if it is locked. She looks through the peephole. There wasn't anyone outside. She darts back to bed, and the shadowy image reappears. This time she didn't yell out. Instead, she snuggled into the quilt, watching and waiting until the image disappeared from the beam of light.

"Good morning," yells Dr. Fairchild through the connecting door.

Dr. Kendall opens the interior door.

"Good morning."

"I am going to order some coffee. Would you like some?" Dr. Fairchild asks.

"Yes, that would be wonderful."

"You are up early," says Dr. Fairchild.

"I have to get to the lab early. Did you find anything in the inspector's notes?"

"Only a speculation of who he thought the killer is."

"You didn't mention this last night."

"No, because there isn't anything to mention. His last entry was a meeting with me the night he was murdered. He stated in his notes that he was to unveil the identity of a suspect at the meeting. But he didn't write his speculation in his notes. No, he kept this a secret from the police department as well. He didn't share this with anyone else."

"This remains a mystery, making everything more convoluted."

"Room service is here."

"Good morning, Miss!" says the room service attendant.

"What's this on the tray?"

"Oh, the flower and note were on the floor outside your room."

"There's blood on the note," says Dr. Fairchild.

"I am sorry. When I picked up the stem, I pricked my finger. Please forgive me."

"Are you okay? It's all right," Dr. Fairchild reassures. "Thank you. Here's your tip."

"Dr. Kendall, would you come here, please?"

"Sure. Mmmm, the coffee smells delightful."

"Please look at this. Someone left me their calling card."

"A long-stemmed black rose," says Dr. Kendall.

"Read the note."

"It's a matter of time before you're mine!" Dr. Kendall reads.

"I checked the hallway. There's no one. And there are no cameras in the hall."

"How convenient. I am going to the lab. I will take these and check for any evidence."

"The blood on the paper isn't mine. It's the room service attendant's. She pricked her finger."

"Did she see anyone?"

"No. I already asked."

"If you don't mind, I will skip the meeting with you and Korey this morning."

"That's understandable. I am going to the gallery. I have a lot to accomplish before the grand opening. I am supposed to have a reception a week before the grand opening. I don't think I will. We are cutting it pretty close, even being ready for the grand opening."

"I should have the results on our new findings by the end of the day. This is a priority. The lab technician will work with me. I am collecting a favor."

"Normally, I would be working on solving this diligently. But I think I am too close."

"I agree. You are human, and it's okay not to be superwoman all the time."

"This is a tough one to figure out."

"Dr. Fairchild, enjoy the gallery. Korey and I can work on this together. Let's meet up for dinner back here at six o'clock. Maybe we can be more congenial than last night."

"I am almost dressed. I will be ready to leave in a few minutes," says Dr. Fairchild.

"Me too. We can leave together. I am glad to be back and working with you. I would like to think that we are more than business colleagues."

"So, when are you moving to Canada?" asks Dr. Fairchild.

"We are more than colleagues, you are a dear friend. I'm not sure if I'll make that move in the near future. We are dear friends, you are someone that I highly respect and admire," replies Dr. Kendall.

Chapter Fifty-Nine

"Interesting. Bailey is opening a gallery. I have always wanted to be more involved in the fine arts. A different take from being rich enough to buy any painting one's heart desires. Now, I have the opportunity to own and run a gallery. One might say that I have too much time on my hands and too much wealth to satisfy all my hunger. I'm in a position to possess the best that money can buy. In time, Dr. Fairchild, you will be mine"

These words are spoken outwardly while she admires her reflection in the mirror.

Chapter Sixty

"Korey, how is everything coming along with transporting the paintings from the warehouse to the gallery?" Dr. Fairchild asks.

"Fine, no problems. Abraham is a remarkable young guy. I spent most of the last two days working with him. He knows art and how to run a gallery."

"I am glad that you like him. It's amazing how more open-minded you have become with Abraham."

"His background check came back clear. With everything that has been going on, I didn't want to take any chances when it comes to your safety."

"And, I appreciate how much you care. I know you are smitten."

"Smitten? Who am I smitten over, if I may ask?"

Dr. Fairchild smiles flirtatiously.

"Me!"

"Oh, really? Are we full of ourselves?"

Korey's tone has been sharp and annoyed with Dr. Fairchild's arrogance. *Maybe I'm annoyed with her because she's right, and I know it's one-sided.*

"Well, I guess I am wrong?"

"It's not a question of being right or wrong. It's how presumptuous you are," Korey retorts.

"For now, I think we better stay focused on the gallery and these cases.".

"I didn't mean to upset you."

"Forget it."

"Korey, look at me. Seriously, I am sorry."

Dr. Fairchild's rosebud lips project a smile that calms his spirit. In return, Korey acknowledges Dr. Fairchild's apology with his boyish charming smile.

"At two o'clock I will be meeting the caterers. Abraham has already met with a photographer, the local newspaper, and with KWYN Channel 3."

"He is ambitious. You were right to make him the gallery manager. He knows the business."

"It feels incredible and sad at the same time that this is happening."

"Why the diverse emotions?"

"The gallery is everything that represents a part of my past and future. Paddy not being here is my sadness."

"I think he will always be with you. He is in your heart and spirit. Is there anything else on today's agenda?"

"The musicians will be here at four o'clock."

"What musicians?"

"They are from the Montreal Symphony."

"You are having a symphony?" Korey asks.

"No, silly, not the entire symphony, only three violinists, a cellist, and a pianist. By the way, the baby grand is being delivered today."

"A piano for the musicians? They can't roll their own to the grand opening?"

"The piano is staying in the gallery. I bought a piano. I want Reflections to have elegance and sophistication. Paddy wanted sophistication, and that is what this gallery will be."

"I suppose we will be greeting the guest with a red carpet."

"Now that you mentioned it, please ask Abraham to order a red carpet with the draperies. Thank you."

"Is there anything else that I need to do or are there other purchases being delivered?"

"No, this is it, for now. Dr. Kendall and I are meeting at six at the hotel for dinner. We would like you to join us to discuss the cases. She is at the medical examiner's lab. Dr. Kendall will need a ride back to the hotel.

"When I finish with Abraham, I will head over to the lab. I will see you both later. One more thing, could you leave after the piano arrives?"

"When is that?"

"Now. The delivery van just pulled up to the back. Please set the piano to the left side of the foyer facing the guest when they walk down the red carpet," Dr. Fairchild points to the exact place for the piano to reside.

"Centered or diagonal?" Korey asks.

"Centered?"

"Centered within the red carpet or centered in the parameters of the foyer?"

"Funny. Just center the damn thing. I'm sure you can figure it out."

Dr. Fairchild is annoyed with Korey's constant childish badgering. She walks away to converse with the caterers.

Dr. Fairchild's discussion with the caterers is interrupted graciously by the beautiful "Für Elise" by Beethoven. The loud commotion of voices whispering and chatting throughout the gallery has come to a dead silence.

Dr. Fairchild shuffles her feet through the crowd that gathered around the piano. The song is beautifully played. Anticipating the pianist, she pushes aggressively through the crowd. Her destination is halted. She gasps for air, astounded by the identity of the mystery pianist. It is Korey playing the song so beautifully. His fingers caress the keys with such elegance. The crowd screams for an encore. Their applause roar throughout the gallery. Korey stood and gave the crowd a bow. The applause grows louder.

"Korey, that was absolutely beautiful. I didn't know you played the piano."

"And I didn't know you could paint."

He kissed her cheek.

"I will see you tonight at the hotel."

He left the gallery with the crowd in awe.

"Dr. Fairchild, I have ordered the red carpet. The gold and red draperies will be delivered with the red carpet. The photographer would like to shoot some black and white shots of the gallery before and after the renovation. His name is Peter Frank. He will be here in one hour."

"Abraham, you are doing an outstanding job. I think this is your forte. I will meet with Mr. Frank when he arrives. At that time, please continue with the caterers."

"How many courses do you want?"

"Five, including the appetizers. At five o'clock, champagne will be served with appetizers; dinner will take place at seven. Does Mr. Frank need to meet with me? The musicians will be here in a few minutes, and I would like to work with them."

"He is only here to shoot."

"If I don't see you before you leave, thank you and have a wonderful evening."

Dr. Fairchild receives a call from Dr. Kendall.

"I will have to meet you at the restaurant. I will be leaving in half an hour. The lab results are taking a little longer than anticipated."

"That's perfect. Korey will meet us at the restaurant. He is running a bit late as well. It will give us a chance to chat and have a glass of wine. I am the farthest away. I am leaving now. We should arrive about the same time."

Dr. Fairchild has completed more than what has been on her agenda. *I am ready to leave. It's been a long and exciting day.*

"I am sorry to intrude Abraham, but I am leaving now. Please set the alarm when you leave. Good night."

"Good night, Dr. Fairchild."

I really like Abraham. It is refreshing that he turned out to be such a nice guy. My heart breaks for Alayna. It's obvious she had some decency within her. She would be proud of Abraham.

Dr. Fairchild arrives a little early.

"Hello, Dr. Fairchild, we have your table ready. Would you like to start with a bottle of cabernet?"

"Pierre, you know me too well. Please, that would be wonderful. The rest of the party will be here momentarily. All of us will be drinking wine."

"Hello."

"Hello, I've ordered a bottle of cabernet. It should be here soon."

Dr. Fairchild and Dr. Kendall exchange hugs as they greet one another.

"You missed a fantastic performance by Korey. He played the piano brilliantly this afternoon."

"Where?"

"At the gallery. I bought a baby grand, the first piece of furniture. He played Beethoven's 'Für Elise.' It was breathtaking. He played as though he was Beethoven himself."

"What's this about Beethoven?" Korey interrupts.

"Hey, I didn't see you sneak up. You are in time for some cabernet."

"It sounded like you didn't see me," he says.

"Bailey was boasting about your brilliant performance this afternoon."

"Could I talk you into playing the 'Für Elise' as the opening song for the grand opening?"

"Yes, just for you." His smile confirms his commitment.

"Bailey and I went over these notes last night, or, should I say, early this morning. This is the results from the DNA that was on the calling card."

"What calling card? May I have the plastic bag?"

Korey holds the evidence plastic bag in the air while reading the contents.

" *'It's a matter of time and you'll be mine.'* What the hell is this?"

"There was a long-stemmed black rose with the note. Both were left at the outside of her door this morning," says Dr. Kendall.

"Whose bloodstain is on the calling card, as you call it?"

"The DNA from the bloodstain is from the room service attendant. She pricked her finger when she picked the rose up."

"Did anybody see anyone?"

"No. We asked that same question," says Dr. Fairchild.

"Where were the police officers? They were supposed to be parked in front of your door."

"I never saw any policemen," says Dr. Fairchild.

"That's unacceptable."

"I will be calling the chief of police. Why didn't you tell me this earlier today? Damn it, Bailey, I wish you weren't so flippant about the danger you are in, not to mention the danger you put Dr. Kendall in. Is there anything else that I should know?" Korey expresses his concerns angrily.

"That's pretty much it, except for the stack of analysis reports and cases that we have to conclude for a conviction."

"The killer is becoming more confident. They have moved themselves to a new level of thrill-seeking at Bailey's expense."

During dinner, Korey's cell phone went off half a dozen times. There is one call that intrigued him enough to excuse himself during dinner.

"Excuse me, please." He moves away from the table. "I need to take this call."

Korey leaves the restaurant.

"What's the urgency that I have to excuse myself from dinner with the girls?" Korey asks Perry.

"Would it be possible for you to meet me tonight?"

"Again, what's the urgency?"

"Give me your word you won't say anything to Bailey about this call. It's regarding Paddy."

Korey knows by Perry's tone that this needed to be addressed.

"All right, I am having dinner with Bailey and Dr. Kendall."

"Seriously, Korey, not a word," Perry demands.

"I promise. I will make my excuse and meet you where?"

"Use your boyish charm on Bailey. Meet me in my office in twenty minutes."

"Excuse me! The boyish charm routine is your gig, not mine," replies Korey.

"Whatever you need to do. It's critical."

Korey returns to the table and takes a deep breath.

"Sorry ladies, I have to leave. Something has come up that I have to resolve this evening with the FBI agent."

Korey leaves two hundred dollars on the table.

"Dinner and the evening are on me. Please order another bottle of wine."

"Thank you, sorry you can't stay. We are almost done. Do you need our help?" Dr. Fairchild asks.

"Please relax and enjoy yourselves. You both need a little fun and it's overdue."

Dr. Fairchild grabs Korey's hand.

"Thank you, call me tomorrow."

Chapter Sixty-One

"Nurse, would you please come here? John Doe has been calling out about the last five minutes," requests the FBI agent stationed outside John Doe's hospital room.

"Just a minute," she replies as she waddles towards him.

"I've told you many times before, it is very normal for coma patients to blurt out."

"I am telling you he didn't blurt out. He spoke clear and loud enough for me to hear him say Anna twice," the FBI agent insists.

"There does seem to be some changes in his vitals."

The nurse rings the nurses station, requesting an urgent page for a doctor on duty. Within a few minutes, Dr. Sheldon appeared.

"What's the urgency?" he asks.

"His vitals are showing an improvement. He whispered something when I was standing next to him," replies the nurse.

"Are you sure it was words, not a sigh?"

"Forgive me for interrupting, but I heard him loud and clear, too."

"Who are you?"

"I am FBI Agent Roux. John Doe called out for Anna twice."

"Well, that does put a different view on the situation."

"Is it a sign that he is coming out of his coma?"

"Not necessarily. It's more complicated. I am not trying to steal any hope, but, medically, I doubt it."

"In layman's words, this sounds like a bunch of bull. Why would he speak clearly and loud enough for me to understand?"

"Listen, Doc, I don't mean to question your expertise, but this man may be involved in one of the most heinous serial killings. So, let's stop beating around the bush and try to get this man talking."

"I understand you have a job to do and so do I. It's not that easy to explain or to understand coma patients. In most coma cases, the patient, if fortunate enough to pull through, may have amnesia. Now, I am telling you to leave. Do not disturb this man."

"I'll be outside. Please let me know if any changes occur. It is still crucial that confidentiality is mandated with all employees."

"That's no problem. In case of any improvements, do you know of any family who should be notified?"

"There is a granddaughter, but she isn't aware of his state. We are trying to keep her safe as well. I will share with you what I can. His assailant was after her. He was in the wrong place at the wrong time. We want her to believe that he is dead in hopes to flush out the serial killer or killers. At this time, we are not sure if the killings are being done only by one person. They have killed others in their path. This is a very dangerous situation. That is why it is crucial that all employees keep this confidential. The less staff who knows, the safer for those involved."

"I am glad you explained the level of urgency. You will have our full cooperation. If there's anything we can do to further assist the FBI, please let us know.

"We know for a fact that if it is made public that he is still alive, it will put his life in jeopardy.

"It seems as though you do know his identity."

"We weren't sure until the district attorney identified him. That's true.

"Now, part of our protection is to have the medical staff and the reporters believe we don't know his identity.

"People talk; this is a smoke screen to give the authorities time to find the killer before another person loses his life...and the possibility the assailant will come back to finish off John Doe. We believe John Doe will be able to identify his assailant if he doesn't have amnesia."

"I understand now. What about his granddaughter's safety?"

"She isn't aware of the twenty-four–hour surveillance team we have on her."

"Why not tell her about John Doe?"

"The FBI doesn't think it would be in their best interest. She is a forensic anthropologist working on this case and two other cases that are linked to this serial killer. He is in a coma, and the distraction of his well-being could cost her life."

"Personally, you feds make some irrational decisions. I think knowing he is alive might save his life. He is barely hanging on. It's a miracle he is even alive. There might be side effects if he even pulls through."

"Exactly my point. All of these maybe too much for her, and we need her emotions to be contained. She is the best in this field."

"Amazing, it's all about the feds cracking a case at anyone's expense."

"You do understand that if anyone, including you, interferes in any way with this investigation, that one will be prosecuted."

"Don't worry, you will have our fullest cooperation."

Chapter Sixty-Two

"Hi, Korey, please come in and have a seat. Thanks for dropping everything. This is important."

"You said it's about Paddy. Did they arrest someone?"

"No. Paddy is alive."

"This isn't the time for any jokes."

"I swear it's the truth."

"Why are you telling me? We should be telling Bailey."

Korey reaches for the phone. Perry pushes his hand away.

"Listen to me. Stop trying to be Bailey's hero."

Korey gets up and starts walking towards the door.

"If you called to have me come here to be insulted, you are wrong. I don't have the time for your games. Again, Bailey must be notified."

"Please listen to me. I am sorry I was a jerk. Enough okay. We both love Bailey and want her best interest. Paddy is in a coma at St. Mary's Hospital. The FBI has a twenty-four–hour surveillance in front of his room."

"The FBI is involved? What happened? I think we'll need a drink for this."

"Scotch on the rocks?"

A bottle of Scotch and two whiskey glasses are displayed decoratively on a mirror tray on the corner of Perry's desk.

"Yes, and make it a double. Thanks."

"After Paddy's assailant left him for dead, he started to vomit, which purged most of the nitroglycerin out. The paramedics immediately pumped his stomach before sending him to the hospital. I know this is bizarre."

Perry hands a glass of scotch to Korey. Perry extends his arm towards Korey to toast their glasses. Korey pulls away.

"I don't think so, this is crap what you put Bailey through," says Korey.

"Prior to the inspector's death, he notified the FBI regarding his concern for Paddy's safety. When he was attacked, the feds stepped in and he has around-the-clock bodyguards."

"Why not tell Bailey? She is heartbroken."

"I know. That's why it kills me to keep her in the dark. The FBI is afraid her life will be in more danger if she knows. Paddy is listed as John Doe at the hospital."

"How did you get involved?"

"You would ask? My relationship with Libby, and her killer is still at large. They believe these two cases are connected, possibly the inspector's case, too."

"How did the FBI connect the two?"

"The inspector who was murdered was investigating Libby's case and was tracking the serial killer. It's a confusing mess. Korey, the inspector wrote in his notes that he can identify the serial killer. He noted that he had a meeting scheduled to see Bailey the night he was murdered."

"Bailey never mentioned a meeting with the inspector."

"The FBI is working with the chief of police. They are scrutinizing everything."

"God, Perry, Bailey is going to lose it, she should know about Paddy. Will I be able to visit Paddy?"

"No, because they are monitoring everyone entering his room. I am not allowed either."

"They really need each other. I am against keeping this from Bailey. Paddy would probably pull through if Bailey was there for him. She is hurting so much. This is barbaric."

"Korey, I have spent hours trying to talk sense into the FBI, but after hearing their reasoning, I agree."

"I don't know their reasoning behind it. This could backfire and then what?"

"What do you mean backfire?"

"That Paddy could die. How do you explain Paddy dying twice? Who did she bury? Furthermore, what twisted game is the FBI playing?

"They are taking advantage of her state of mind. The worst part of all of these, they are still trying to convince her that his death was accidental."

"Hey, Korey, calm down, we are in this together," says Perry.

"For the record, we are not in this together. How much did they pay the ME to participate in this bullshit?

"And what about you, Perry, what are they paying you, or better yet, did they give you immunity from Libby's murder? This seems surreal."

"Enough, Korey, the accusations are not necessary or warranted."

"I am out of here. I will do everything in my power to find this bloody killer. You're a disgrace, Perry."

Korey is embroiled in a deadly race to find out the truth to save Dr. Fairchild.

Chapter Sixty-Three

"Good morning, Korey, is everything okay?" Dr. Kendall asks. "You left last night in such a hurry."

"Yes, everything is fine."

"Are you available to meet me this morning for coffee? I have DNA results from the calling card that was left for Bailey. I would like to discuss the results with you. It's important."

"Sure. The restaurant in your hotel would be best. Bailey will be at the gallery at nine."

"I will see you in an hour."

Korey decides to walk the five blocks to the hotel where he is meeting Dr. Kendall. He is hoping that the crisp air and the walk will snap him out of his foul mood, a residue from the disappointing meeting he had with Perry the night before.

"Good morning. I hope you don't mind, I took the liberty and ordered coffee."

"That's fine," says Korey.

"I have two plastic evidence bags with the same type of DNA from two different crime scenes. In bag A, there are two strands of hair: one strand indicates the person dyed her hair; the other, no hair dye, meaning, their natural hair color. In bag B, one strand, no hair dye. It would be impossible to dye your hair and leave one strand untouched," says Dr. Kendall.

"Do you know who the person is?"

"Yes, Bailey."

"Bailey!"

"I know that the strand with no dye is Bailey's. She has never dyed her hair. The second one with the dye has the same DNA. I did a more intense testing and there is a slight difference in the DNA."

"What does this mean?"

"Brace yourself, it's hard to believe. There's a possibility that Bailey has an identical twin. This is the missing piece to the puzzle. If this is true, Bailey's identical twin is the serial killer."

Korey's cell phone rings.

"Hello." No answer.

"Hello, Bailey, did you just call?" No response; he only hears her voice mail.

"Dr. Kendall, I don't think there is enough evidence to state that Bailey has an identical twin. I am going to her condo to make sure she is okay."

"I thought she wasn't allowed to be there?"

"She isn't allowed. But the phone number that appeared on my cell phone is her home number."

"Be careful."

Korey drives through a couple of red lights, racing to get to Dr. Fairchild's condo. His nerves are on the edge, a mixture of the mysterious phone call from Dr. Fairchild's place and Dr. Kendall's discovery. He pulls into the driveway.

"Sir, sir," a lady shouts while crossing the street, holding a gruffly ball of fur.

"How can I help you?"

"I have seen you here before. Well, this is Dr. Fairchild's cat, Mousey. Dr. Fairchild asked me to keep an eye out for her. Mousey loves to come over and play with my Henry. He is a beautiful and smart Snowshoe Siamese. My Henry has four white paws and a white bib as an undercoat."

Korey is annoyed by this woman's loquacious behavior. Korey walks away from the woman, making his way towards the front door.

"Sir, I saw Dr. Fairchild last night."

He turns away from the condo, walking towards Ms. Chatty Kathy.

A woman hiding in the condo furtively peeks through the venetian blinds inside the condo. "No, no you gorgeous creature, come back," she softly says.

Her face snarls of agony as she rotates the butcher knife blade from one side to the other in the palm of her hand. She speaks in disappointment. *That damn noisy neighbor.*

"Ma'am, I don't mean to be rude, but I can't take the cat. I will have Dr. Fairchild come for her later this week."

Korey attempts to retract himself back to the condo. He pauses. He remembers part of her conversation, but wants avowal.

"Miss, what did you say about last night?" he asks the obnoxious neighbor.

"Oh, please, call me Beatrice. I am too old to be called 'Miss.' My husband would be offended."

"Beatrice, please I am in a hurry."

"Well, I saw Dr. Fairchild pace back and forth across the catwalk in her condo. You know, those big windows, there's no privacy. You can see everything. I told George, my husband, that we should take Mousey to her. I tried calling, but she didn't answer."

"What time did you see Dr. Fairchild?"

"Let me think. It was 8:30?

"Are you sure?"

"Young man, you need to use your manners, and not be in such a rush. Definitely, George, every night, has ice cream at 8:30. It's our tradition. You, young people, might want to incorporate more tradition in your life and less running around."

Korey kisses Beatrice on the forehead.

"Thank you, and I am sorry for my abruptness. You're a gem."

The noisy neighbor just saved your life, the mystery woman in the condo thinks.

* * *

Dr. Kendall was right about a possible identical twin. I have to talk to Paddy. This is still speculation. I need proof. These are Korey's thoughts.

Korey realizes he can't ask anyone in the hospital about the whereabouts of Paddy. Luckily, the hospital only has two floors. There was an FBI agent seated to the left of Paddy's door. Interestingly, he was asleep. A nurse kicks the agent's chair, startling him from his nap, making him feel embarrassed that he has been caught sleeping on the job. A few words has been exchanged between them before the agent walks to the restroom. Korey takes advantage of this opportunity. He quietly slithers into Paddy's room, unseen.

"Mr. Fairchild, I am Korey Scott. Please forgive me for disturbing you. I hope you can hear me. I am a colleague of Bailey's, and she is a dear friend. I need your help. Bailey's life is in mortal danger. We believe the killer is her twin, but we don't have enough proof."

There is no response from Paddy. He lies still, there's no flinching, no reaction to his granddaughter's possible demise.

"This was a bad idea. I am so sorry."

"Hey, where are you going?" says Paddy.

"I was going to leave." A startled Korey approaches Paddy's bedside.

"Please stay, we have to talk. I've been pretending that I am still in a coma."

"Why didn't you let the doctors know you were okay?"

"By letting them think I was in a coma, I learned a lot from the agent and the doctor's conversations. It's amazing how much people say around you when they think you can't hear. The one thing that has kept me silent until now is Bailey's life. And...you must call me Paddy."

"Do you remember what happened to you or who attacked you?"

"No, that's another reason why I stayed quiet."

"How are you feeling?"

"A little disoriented; I will be okay. I am more concerned about Bailey. You know she is going to be furious when she finds out. She doesn't like surprises. Why are you involved? Most colleagues don't risk their own neck. They have the authorities take over. You are in love with her, I can tell."

"How did you know?"

"It's in your eyes, your voice. You glow when you say her name. Displaying that much emotion means one thing—love, deep love."

"Yes, I am in love with her. I am not sure the feelings are mutual."

"Don't give up on her. She will come around. Trust me, I know my granddaughter."

"What do we do now?" Korey asks.

"We play the game even if it means I have to continue this charade for a while. I agree with the FBI. Keeping Bailey in the dark will keep her safe," replies Paddy.

"Some news to brighten your day. Bailey is opening a gallery in Montreal. The grand opening is in two days. She has designed a state-of-the-art gallery."

"She made her dream come true. I am proud of her," says Paddy.

"Paddy, does Bailey have an identical twin?"

"Yes, but she died at childbirth."

"It doesn't seem that way. If not, then we have one hell of a copycat serial killer."

"What do you mean serial killer? You're serious about Bailey being in mortal danger. So, you are telling me she may have been the person who tried to kill me, as well as harming Bailey?"

"Yes, a real strong possibility. She has already killed two people Bailey's assistant and an inspector. She has left threatening notes. My gut feeling is she is done playing cat and mouse with Bailey. Her next move will be to kill Bailey soon."

"Are they identical?"

"Yes."

"Do you remember leaving clues? Bailey said it was a game you two played when she was a little girl."

"I am sorry I don't remember."

"Will you be able to carry on as a coma patient for a couple of more days?"

"That will be easy."

"I have a plan but only if you are strong enough. I would like you at the grand opening. Having you there would be the icing on the cake. I will rent you a penguin suit. I think we are about the same size."

"Korey, I don't want the shock of seeing me upset Bailey on her special moment."

"She will be so happy to see you. It won't matter. That will enhance the evening."

"I like your plan."

"See you soon."

Korey sneaks out of Paddy's room and heads down the stairwell. *It's too late to call Dr. Kendall.*

Chapter Sixty-Four

"Where have you been?"

Half asleep, Korey drops the phone.

"Hello, who is it?"

"Korey, it's Bailey. I haven't seen or heard from you. Are you okay?"

He answers, his voice groggy from snoring.

"Yeah, just extra busy at the gallery."

"Abraham said he hasn't seen you."

"I've been in and out of the gallery and working with Dr. Kendall at the lab."

"Any breaking news?"

"No," replies Korey.

"The grand opening will be in a couple of days."

"That's wonderful. I have to ask you something. When did you put your condo up for sale?"

"Last Saturday. How did you find out?"

"I went over to the condo yesterday. You called my cell. When I answered, you hung up. Caller ID showed your condo phone number."

"Korey, I never called you. I haven't been at the condo in a couple of weeks. My last visit was to get some clothes and toiletries. I am leaving the furniture there until it is bought. I decided that going back there would be too difficult after what transpired between Libby and Perry at the condo. There are too many bad memories. I need a new start."

"There is some good news. Your neighbor across the street has Mousey."

"Oh, that's fantastic news. I'll go pick her up later today."

"That won't be necessary. I've already made arrangements with Abraham. The hotel will allow Mousey to stay with you under these circumstances."

"Thank you. You have thought of everything. When is Abraham picking Mousey up?"

"As we speak, he is bringing Mousey back to the gallery. We wanted to surprise you."

"How can I ever pay you back? You have been a dear friend, and I've been a bitch. I…thank you again."

I almost said I love you, are her thoughts.

"When are you coming to the gallery?"

"I was planning this afternoon. I am meeting Dr. Kendall. She has been working diligently on these cases. Her work ethics are a lot like yours."

"I will see you later then."

Chapter Sixty-Five

"Dr. Kendall, this is Korey. I hope I am not calling too early. You are right. Bailey has an identical twin."

"How can you be so sure? It makes sense why Bailey has been the person of interest; explains how her DNA was found at every crime scene when she was in a different part of the country."

"There's something else. Paddy is alive."

"Are you sure?"

"Yes, Paddy is at St. Mary's Hospital. He was in a coma. I talked with him last night. He confirms that Bailey had an identical twin, but she died during childbirth, he thought."

"God, Korey, this means Bailey's sister is a serial killer. How does anyone break this kind of news to her? She killed Libby and the inspector. She thinks she killed Paddy."

"The most frightening part, she's wants Bailey."

"When do we tell Bailey?" Dr. Kendall asks.

"We can't. The FBI is involved. I am not even supposed to know. To keep her safe, we can't tell her about Paddy. Our first obligation is to convict her sister. It won't be easy."

"I think if the FBI knows what we do, it might make it easier for them."

"Maybe. I think for the time being, keeping Paddy dead will keep Bailey alive."

"Have you noticed how Bailey has been kept at bay with these cases? They're too close to her emotionally. I don't think she could handle finding out she has an identical sister; her own flesh and blood, a serial killer. What irony? Bailey has been chasing a sister she never knew existed. Obviously, her sister knows that Bailey is her identical twin. Why would she want to kill Bailey? What extremely different personalities," says Dr. Kendall.

"Opening this gallery has been her sanctuary. She has been handling Paddy's loss pretty well," says Korey.

"Korey, you can't try to be a knight in shining armor for Bailey. Pursuing her sister is a suicide mission. She is a monster."

"I promise you I won't be doing anything, at least, for now."

"I will be running more tests on the evidence. I am going to study the inspector's report one more time. We must have missed something that can convict her sister. Did Paddy recognize his killer?" Dr. Kendall asks.

"No, Paddy has no memory of the attack."

"It's normal to lose short-term memory."

"Will he ever remember?"

"Possibly, but it's hard to say when."

"His memory would convict the killer."

"We need concrete evidence, in case he doesn't remember."

"Regardless, let's do what we can to ensure that the grand opening is a sensation for Bailey."

"If the killer is Bailey's sister, my heart goes to her. What I mean is the pain, agony, whatever has caused the woman's evil to surface. It is sad. I would like to know what ordeal transformed her personality into such a coldhearted being," Dr. Kendall states.

"You're right, it is sad."

"It's getting late. I have to stop by the gallery to see if there are any last minute honeydews before the grand opening."

"You are a good friend. She is very fortunate to have you in her life."

"Dr. Kendall, thanks for everything, mostly for working with me in confidence."

"Unless there's more for us to accomplish, I'll see you tomorrow evening. Don't forget, it's black and white tie attire," says Dr. Kendall.

"Oh, great, a tuxedo," he replies sarcastically.

Chapter Sixty-Six

"Hey, beautiful. Wow! The gallery is breathtaking. The statue of David in the foyer sets the ambiance."

"You really like it?"

"It's impressive and well-done. The best of the best is displayed throughout the gallery with elegance and grace. You are gifted with many talents. It's put together with perfection. Every piece of artwork, whether it be a painting or a statue, seduces your heart. Nice touch with tapestry."

"I like the concept of seducing one's heart," says Dr. Fairchild.

"Abraham is a godsend. If it wasn't for him, Reflections wouldn't be opening tonight."

"Are you nervous?"

"Yes...and excited; I feel guilty to be so happy. It is so soon after Paddy's death. Shouldn't I be in mourning instead of rejoicing?"

"That is ridiculous. Your grandfather would prefer you being happy. The gallery is in his honor. Enjoy!"

"Did you get a tux?"

"Yes."

"Please don't be so enthused."

"The thought of looking like a penguin makes me real enthused." Korey gravels.

"Are you nervous to perform in front of a large crowd?"

"It's amazing what we trained penguins can do?"

"Smart ass," replies Dr. Fairchild.

"More like a clown."

"Thank you for the gorgeous corsage. It was a sweet thought. I love it."

"What time are you planning to be at the gallery?"

"I have to be here at four o'clock. The cocktail reception is at five. I want to be here for the guests who will arrive early."

"I will be here at four as well."

"I am going to leave. I have to start getting ready. It takes a woman longer to get ready."

"When are you leaving?"

"Probably in an hour. I need to practice. I will check with Abraham for any last minute issues that may arise."

Chapter Sixty-Seven

The tranquility of a hot bubble bath haunts Dr. Fairchild's mind a thousand times.

"Thank you for the door service."

Dr. Fairchild leaves the taxi. The hotel is unusually quiet, eerie to say the least, except for the reservation clerk. Dr. Fairchild has felt a foreboding essence in the lobby. There isn't anyone. Dr. Fairchild is pleased that the room service had her evening dress dry-cleaned. The aroma welcomes Dr. Fairchild when she enters the room. The plastic garment bag hang graciously over the door featuring a gold satin chiffon long dress.

Dr. Fairchild pours an extra capful of the lavender bath minerals into the hot bath water. The blend of the oil and bubbles gave a scent of enchantment. The hot water turns her pale white skin to a soft pink. She closes her eyes, allowing her body to sink further into the depths of the water. The steam is overwhelming with mist, making each breath a challenge. As much as she wants to continue her enchanted moment of tranquility, time is limited. Dr. Fairchild wraps a towel around her statuesque body, wiping off any bubbles that were caressing her skin. Halfway in a daze, Dr. Fairchild gingerly walks to the other room to start a new portrait. Her attire will be a masterpiece.

"Oh, my God!" Dr. Fairchild screams, her eyes transfixed with horror.

Her dress is neatly draped over the bed. Dr. Fairchild doesn't see anyone in the room. She checks the closet. It's empty. *Am I losing my mind? I don't have time for this. I have to get dressed.*

Dr. Fairchild steps into the satin gown and pulls the sleeveless top onto her bare shoulders, accentuating her elegant physique. She slips on the gold satin shoes. Dr. Fairchild removes a pearl necklace from a jewelry case. She arranges the pearls to lie across her collarbone. The final touch is the white satin gloves caressing over her long thin fingers.

Chapter Sixty-Eight

"Korey, this black rose and note were left at the back door for Dr. Fairchild," says Abraham.

"Did you see anyone?"

"No. I was the only one in the back."

"Thanks, Abraham."

Korey read the note, *"You will not be attending the grand opening, I will."*

The guests are arriving. There's no sign of Dr. Fairchild.

"Korey, have you seen Bailey?" Dr. Kendall asks.

"I haven't. She is forty-five minutes late. This is not like her."

"I have a surprise for her. Paddy will be here. He is doing incredibly well."

"Has he been released from the hospital?" Dr. Kendall asks. "We are keeping the FBI in the dark."

"No. We have a plan. He will sneak out. I have prearranged for Abraham to drive Paddy to my hotel to get ready, and then to the warehouse. Paddy's full attire is in the room."

"You boys have been making plans. Does he remember anything about his incident?"

"Still nothing. That is why we are keeping it quiet that he is out of his coma. He has been for weeks."

"All this time he was okay? What was the purpose?"

"Paddy said when he was believed to be in a coma, he learned quite a bit from the doctors and the FBI about his assailant. Once he realized that Bailey's life is in danger, he played the game," says Korey.

"Dr. Kendall, will you be able to stall the party for a while? Give them some champagne; that should keep them happy. I am going to the hotel. This is not like her. Bailey is never late. She would have called by now. On my way out, I am going to text Paddy to confirm that he is going.

"Paddy doesn't have a phone in his room. I bought him a cell phone. We have been texting back and forth. Matter of fact, he is texting me right now. He is going to the grand opening, but he is running late. He said the Model T Ford doesn't go very fast. It's a guarantee he won't be pulled over for speeding."

"Is he okay?"

Paddy texts, *"Korey...Do you want me to still escort you and Bailey this evening in the Model T Ford?*

Korey texts, *"When you leave the hospital, call me, urgent."*

Chapter Sixty-Nine

Dr. Fairchild puts the final touch to her hair, pleased that the attire she created for the evening is a masterpiece that will turn heads. Her moment of admiration is interrupted. The curtains that adorn the front of the sliding glass door slightly swayed from a breeze. Dr. Fairchild doesn't recall opening the door. She reaches to pull back the curtains, horrified by her unexpected encounter.

"Please, join me. It's a beautiful evening," says a woman from the balcony. Bailey fumbles, trying to flip the light switch on.

"That's not necessary."

Intrigued by this mystery, Dr. Fairchild walks onto the balcony, engrossed by the vision in front of her, speechless and motionless.

"You are not looking at a ghost. I am your identical twin, Rachel Ralston."

"I don't know what to say," Dr. Fairchild cries out, her voice raw with terror.

Dr. Fairchild notices the gun that Rachel is gripping next to her side. It is pointing in her direction.

"I don't understand. Why are you here? Why the gun?"

"Your life is going to become mine," says Rachel.

Dr. Fairchild starts to back up into the room.

"I wouldn't do that. I will shoot."

Rachel tosses an envelope on the table.

"Read this, sis. This is the envelope that Mr. Wade gave you. The one you haven't been able to find."

"I thought I misplaced it. What's inside?"

"No. I removed the envelope from your purse. Looking identical has made everything I did easy. I was the one who laid the red night gown on your bed in Atlantic City. Also, I put the dress you are wearing on the bed during your bubble bath."

Dr. Fairchild notices that Rachel is wearing the exact same dress, shoes, gloves, and accessories.

"What do you mean everything you did? What did you do?"

"Does the name Dr. Charles Ralston mean anything to you?"

"No, not off the top of my head. I am sorry I don't remember a Dr. Charles Ralston."

"Five years ago, you gave a lecture at the University of Toronto. My husband, Dr. Ralston, was to speak at your lecture. He is a forensic anthropologist. Charles made arrangements to meet with you to discuss his wife having an identical twin. Charles never mentioned his discovery to me. I found this out when I had to go through his e-mails. It was like opening Pandora's Box. I e-mailed your assistant as my duty as a widow to inform you that Charles wouldn't be participating at your lecture."

"You said 'widow.' When did he die?"

"The day he was flying to your lecture. Both my husband and son were killed."

"Your son!"

"Anthony received notification from Harvard that he was accepted two days before their trip. He was our only child."

Dr. Fairchild is feeling nauseous and dismayed.

"I am so terribly sorry about your losses. What does this have to do with me?"

"Please, I don't want your sympathy."

"Then what do you want?"

"Already told you what I want, your life."

"How did you get in?"

"I went to the front desk, told them I was Dr. Fairchild, and said that I left my key in the room. That's exactly what I did in Atlantic City. It really has been easy getting away with so much portraying you. There have been many occasions that I have been in your room, watching you. I read your journals. It was me who spilt coffee on a page. I kept you dancing.

"Because of you they are dead. I wanted to make sure you feel the pain of losing someone you dearly love. Losing my family was unbearable. I had a nervous breakdown. I was in a mental hospital until a year ago. The pain never goes away. It just sits there gnawing through the lining in your gut. A constant reminder of what you took away from me."

"Rachel let's talk this through? We are sisters, but I didn't know you existed. What happened to your family is awful, but not my fault."

"There isn't anything you can say that will change my mind. I enjoyed watching you and the agony you were going through during your losses."

Rachel pushes the envelope towards Dr. Fairchild.

"Read the contents. It'll give you a new perspective on our grandfather."

"You know Paddy?" a frightened Dr. Fairchild asks.

"Like I said, looking like you made it easy."

Dr. Fairchild removes two documents.

"Yes. One is my birth certificate and the other is my death certificate. According to Paddy at my last visit with him, I was stillborn and was presumed to be buried with our mother.

"But I guess you could say, fate stepped in. The nurse felt me move in her arms. I was gasping for air. She was approached by a wealthy friend who was looking to adopt a baby girl, an oil tycoon in Texas. My parents were good to me. They never told me I was adopted. I didn't know until after losing my family. Ironically, my parents were killed in my father's plane ten years ago."

"God, your hate and grudge isn't worth killing over," states Dr. Fairchild.

"That's too late. I killed Libby."

"Why? She didn't do you any harm."

"Libby wasn't on my hit list. She should have left the district attorney alone. Libby was perfect to help frame you. She had a strange obsession to be you."

"You didn't answer my question. How do you know Paddy?"

"I went to his house the day he died. At first, he thought I was his precious Bailey. He really adores you."

Dr. Fairchild lunges towards Rachel.

"Did you kill him?"

"Yes, and with pleasure."

"You sick bitch."

"Why do you think you have been marked the person of interest? It was so pathetically easy to frame you. I was intrigued by the fact that I was able to stay ahead of the notorious forensic expert."

"What else did you do?"

"I had to kill the inspector. He was planning to tell you about me. He knew too much. It was me who shot the round of bullets in the lab in Atlantic City. The inspector was in the hall. I removed his cigar butts from the trash and planted them around outside of the lab."

"You could have killed us."

"Believe me, there has been many times when I could have killed you. Watching you squirm out of fear, seeing the pain in your eyes, especially after Paddy's death."

"You could have Paddy and me as family."

"No. The only family that was mine is dead. I will be you and you will be me, but dead. Bailey, Libby disgusted me."

"Killing these people didn't bring your husband and son back. They were innocent."

"And so was my husband and son," replies Rachel.

Rachel steps back in a stance position and raises the gun towards Dr. Fairchild.

This is the only chance I have to make a move.

Dr. Fairchild pushes the table into Rachel. Rachel loses her balance, she falls into the rail. The rail breaks, flipping Rachel over the balcony wall. Dr. Fairchild runs over to Rachel. Rachel is hanging on to the pole that connects the rail to the wall.

"Grab onto my arm," Dr. Fairchild yells.

Rachel pulls Dr. Fairchild's arm towards her aggressively. Their white gloves make it impossible to grip. She clings to Dr. Fairchild's glove. Unable to hang on, the glove slides off, tangling in her hand. Rachel grabs the pearl necklace on Dr. Fairchild, pulling her farther over the wall.

Dr. Fairchild struggles with Rachel. The string of pearls break, flowing down twelve floors.

"Stop it, Rachel, quit fighting me. Please let me pull you up. Come on, grab my arm," pleads Dr. Fairchild.

They stare at each other for a slight moment. Rachel gives a smile. Dr. Fairchild's tear ripples down her cheek. Rachel slowly blinks. She pushes Dr. Fairchild away.

"Forgive me! I must be with my family."

Rachel falls silently to her death twelve floors down. Her body lands in a fetal position.

Dr. Fairchild pulls herself back onto the floor of the balcony, weeping with grief. Dr. Fairchild stays in a coil position, trembling uncontrollably from fear.

Korey breaks down the door to Dr. Fairchild's room. He runs to the balcony.

"Bailey, are you okay?"

He wraps his penguin jacket around her shoulders and escorts her into the room.

"The serial killer was my sister, my identical sister. She killed Paddy, Libby, and the inspector. I didn't know she existed."

Korey wipes her hair from her face.

"I know. Dr. Kendall figured this out. But we only had a suspicion, no facts."

"She was like Alayna. Both were victims of circumstances. Korey, when Rachel was telling me everything, I could see in her eyes that she was truly a wonderful person. The pain that was inflicted by the loss of her husband and only child caused her to snap. I tried to talk her out of killing me. I told her she had a sister, we were family now.

"She wanted me to hurt as much as she was."

"Why you? What did you do?"

"Her husband and son were killed in a plane crash the day he was flying to participate in my lecture. This all started five years ago.

"The saddest part of all of this, she killed Paddy instead of getting to know him. He would have loved her, too. There was me as well. I would have loved to have a sister. God, Korey, this hurts so much."

"Excuse me, I am sorry to interrupt your conversation. Dr. Fairchild, I am FBI Agent Roux. We met a couple of weeks ago. I am here because Mr. Scott was stuck in traffic. He called me for assistance. He said your life was in danger. I gave him an escort to get here. Sorry we didn't make it sooner. I will need a statement. Are you okay?"

"I am a little shaken up. Rachel Ralston, my identical twin sister, was on the balcony the whole time I was getting ready. I didn't know she was here until she called me to go outside. Korey, she brutally murdered two people in my life. She killed the inspector, and I was next."

"Dr. Fairchild, I understand you have a grand opening to go to?

"What about my statement and Rachel?"

"Did I hear you correctly? She is your identical twin?" The FBI agent scratches his head out of disbelief.

"We didn't know each other until now, or, should I say, I didn't know about her until this evening. She has been stalking me the last five years. Inspector, I have one request."

"What's that?"

"Please don't put it in your report that she is a monster. She was a loving wife and mother. I know it doesn't justify or excuse what she did, but she was sick. She told me she was in a mental institution for a nervous breakdown. I don't want her crucified in the newspapers either."

"Dr. Fairchild, I will do my best to protect her. The statement can wait until tomorrow. Get out of here and enjoy the event. I'll try and make it."

"Thank you."

"Korey, I must look a mess."

"You are stunning. I would suggest you leave the other glove here, one's missing."

"In the closet is my cape."

Korey wraps the white velvet cape around her shoulders and kisses her neck. Her perfume excites him.

"Gorgeous, I have a surprise for you."

"What kind of a surprise?"

"You'll see."

They walk out of the hotel lobby. Lights and sirens circle around Rachel's lifeless body. Korey hurdles Dr. Fairchild to the opposite direction of the crime scene.

"Is that the surprise? You drove the Model T Ford. It looks like a car that Bonnie and Clyde would drive."

He pulls Dr. Fairchild toward him, kisses her satin lips, and tells her, "Don't be mad. I love you. The car is only part of the surprise."

"Okay."

"There's a chauffeur."

Korey opens the door. Dr. Fairchild slides onto the leather seat.

"Good evening, Snowbird. You are gorgeous and a sight for sore eyes," says the chauffeur.

"What did you say?"

The voice is familiar to her. The chauffeur turns around facing Dr. Fairchild.

Dr. Fairchild cries, weeps, and throws her arms around the chauffeur.

"Paddy, Paddy is it really you?"

"It's me, Snowbird. Forgive us. We had to let you believe I was dead. There is so much to tell you. May we tell you after the grand opening?"

Dr. Fairchild hugs Korey.

"Are we ready to go to a ball?" Paddy asks.

Dr. Fairchild leans onto Korey, glares at him, almost resentful, then smiles with delight.

"You, sir, have some explaining to do," she tells Korey.

Dr. Fairchild is bewildered by all the events that have transpired. Paddy parks the Model T Ford in front of the gallery. The passenger door is parallel to the red carpet. The three stood in front of the gallery, staring in awe.

"Paddy, I named the gallery after the portrait I painted of Nannie—'Reflections,'—your favorite painting."

"I am so proud of you. Does this mean you are retiring?"

"Maybe so."

"Does this mean you will move to Canada and live with me?" Dr. Fairchild asks.

"Maybe so."

Dr. Fairchild embraces her arm into Paddy's, holds him close to her side, and smiles.

"I love you so much."

"Me too, Snowbird."

Dr. Kendall greets the three musketeers in the foyer.

"Dr. Kendall, I would like you to meet Paddy."

"What a pleasure to meet you, sir."

Paddy, Korey, and Dr. Kendall watch Dr. Fairchild in her element. Glowing with joy, she converses with the guests.

"I am FBI Agent Anderson. I would like to talk to Dr. Fairchild about a case. Do you know where I can find her?"

"She's next to the Mona Lisa, wearing a white cape," says Paddy.

Korey stares at her. *She is so beautiful. Every move she makes is with grace and elegance.* These thoughts fill his heart with happiness.

"The gallery is her niche," says Paddy.

"Do you think she will retire?" Korey asks.

"You tell me. Look at her light up talking to the FBI agent. I don't think he's discussing any paintings. He doesn't look the artsy type."

"I am going to wander over to Bailey. The agent has left," Paddy states.

"Bailey, dear, this is phenomenal. I am not surprised. This is you. May I ask what the FBI agent wanted?"

"There is a case in which he would like our assistance and expertise."

"Our...oh, yes, that includes Korey."

"I was hoping you would live with me and oversee the gallery."

"I would be honored to run the gallery. And now that I'm going to live with you, we will have to think about that."

"What's there to think about?"

"Because I believe Korey would love to spend the rest of his life with you."

"He hasn't suggested that."

Paddy winks at Dr. Fairchild.

"All in time, Snowbird."

Chapter Seventy

Dr. Fairchild kneels next to the new headstone. Each blade of grass is damp from the morning dew. She wipes the wet grass from her clothes.

"Good morning, may I help you up?" Paddy asks.

"Good morning, thank you," Dr. Fairchild extends her arm so Paddy may lift her from the dampness.

"Korey told me that I would find you here. What a beautiful gesture, adding Rachel to your mother's headstone."

"She was my sister. I am sorry things turned out the way they did. I miss not having the chance to love and know her."

"I feel the same way. We both were cheated."

"All three of us were."

"I didn't have any dates engraved on the headstone, only Baby Rachel. That's all she was to us."

"Rachel is buried with her husband and son. I believe that is the appropriate thing to do. She loved them more than her own life. It says a lot about her."

Dr. Fairchild and Paddy close their eyes for a silent prayer. She tenderly holds Paddy's hand.

"Come on, you have some explaining to do," says Dr. Fairchild.

"Like what?" Paddy boyishly plays innocent.

"Don't play innocent with me."

"Well, I only have to say one thing. Korey is a great catch."

"Good try, we are not changing the subject."

"No, let's not change the subject. Good try. Bailey, I love you, but you can be a royal pain in the butt. You are so afraid of getting close to anyone."

"Except with you."

"I know, and that isn't healthy. I am flattered. Please consider letting your guard down and let him in your heart."